Subjunctive Moods

Stories

C.G. MENON

First published 2018 by Dahlia Publishing Ltd
6 Samphire Close Hamilton
Leicester LE5 1RW
ISBN 9780995634435

Copyright © C. G. Menon 2018

The moral right of the author has been asserted.

All rights reserved. No part of this publication may be reproduced, stored in or introduced into a retrieval system, or transmitted, in any form, or by any means (electronic, mechanical, photocopying, recording or otherwise) without the prior written permission of the publisher. Any person who does any unauthorized act in relation to this publication may be liable to criminal prosecution and civil claims for damages.

Some of the stories in this collection have appeared elsewhere, in a slightly different form:

'The Ampang Line' in *Bare Fiction*, 'Subjunctive Moods' in *The Bridport Prize Anthology*, 'Aunty ' in *Leicester Writes Short Story Prize Anthology*, 'Watermelon Seeds' in *Love Across A Broken Map*, 'For You Are Julia' in *The Lonely Crowd*, 'Clay For Bones' in *The Short Story Prize*, 'Dust and Spices' in *The University of Winchester Writers' Festival Best of 2015*, 'Foxgloves' in *Still Life: Birmingham*, 'I See You In Triplicate', Peacocks' in *Baubles*, 'Daylight Savings' in *F(r)iction*, 'Seascapes' in *Fugue Vol. II*, 'Rock Pools' in *Willesden Herald New Short Stories 8*

Printed and bound by Grosvenor Group

This book is sold subject to the condition that it shall not, by way of trade or otherwise, be lent, re-sold, hired out, or otherwise circulated without the publisher's prior consent in any form of binding or cover other than that in which it is published and without a similar condition including this condition being imposed on the subsequent purchaser.

A CIP catalogue record for this book is
available from The British Library

CONTENTS

The Ampang Line	1
Subjunctive Moods	10
Aunty	21
Watermelon Seeds	31
So Long, So Long	44
For You Are Julia	56
Clay for Bones	65
The Names of Things	75
Dust and Spices	87
Foxgloves	96
I See You in Triplicate	105

Peacocks	114
Daylight Savings	128
Farne Islands	139
Seascapes	149
Rock Pools	159
Acknowledgements	
About the Author	

The Ampang Line

"Excited, Shalini?" Dilip shifts up a gear and all the ghosts crowded into the back seat rock together and nod their invisible heads. Not, of course, that they're truly ghosts. Miss Working-Late, Miss Tennis-Partner, Miss She's-Just-A-Friend-My-God-Shalini-Give-It-A-Rest – they're all very much alive and fleshy, going home right now on the Ampang Line and crossing their legs at retired businessmen. But somehow, they're here too. Long hair drips from their perfect skulls and they blow fanged kisses to me in the rear-view mirror. Not ghosts, then – not with those sharpened teeth – but pontianaks. I've conjured up a carful of women bent on revenge.

"Looking forward to seeing what they've done with the old place?" He leans back, spreading his thighs across the seat.

The old place. The old girl. Since he retired he's taken to this bluff, beery way of talking, a sort of permanent slap on the back. He's never even seen the house – after my father died, Elsie sold out to a resort chain and came to our wedding in diamonds – but that doesn't stop him oozing a genial boredom with it all. He's never seen these landslips we're passing, or the mining villages that trail by on cords of mud, but he doesn't bother to give them a second glance.

New things don't ask for much effort, after all. It's the old ones that are tricky.

He spins the steering wheel with the heel of one hand, and we turn into a driveway that feels both familiar and strange at once. A noticeboard hangs at the front among a shorn clump of bougainvillea. Mountainside Hotel, it reads, in curlicued script fresh out of the tin.

The house is unrecognisable, angles and glass polished smooth as Miss Working-Late's knees. I remember a thicket of hibiscus shoots and dizzying deep-water ponds where the mineshafts used to flood. That's all gone now, replaced with a sterile birdbath in a lake of lawn and a lap pool scrubbed chemical blue. Dilip grunts with satisfaction as he glides the car into a painted parking space. It's the sort of arrangement he likes; everything laid out with the crusts cut off.

Inside there's a hygienic lobby, sliced from the garden by tinted windows. Behind all that smoked glass is a little simmer in the ground; a seepage where the ponds are trickling back. They used to overflow, juicy with weed and seething with the monstrous shoals of koi my father bred. Koi are lucky, Elsie once said, when we were still on speaking terms. Before the diamonds, before the disappearance of her ring, before someone draped the mineshafts with grass and buried the fish under a birdbath with their luck gone for good and all.

"The room's ready, Shalini," Dilip calls. A beautiful girl sits behind the reception desk wearing a badge saying "Call me

Adelia", and he looks as though he might just do it. He doesn't seem to quite belong, here in this chilly space where I remember jambu floorboards and striped curtains to hide all our secrets. For a moment I see my father kneeling with an opal ring and Elsie with Chinese pomade in her crisping hair and a smile that spreads like butter. Don't get too attached to that ring, Elsie, it ends up at the bottom of the pond and you never quite forgive any of us. Poor Elsie, she'd have been better off with the pontianaks.

"Up the staircase, madam." The lacquered receptionist smiles with a flickering politeness, the kind that will run out any time soon. Behind her, Dilip's busy with our forms, his head bowed with such immaculate concentration that I almost send the ghosts packing and forgive him on the spot. But then Adelia leans over the mirrored desk and her lovely reflection swims up into his empty hands like a fish with luck knotted tight to its tail.

The bedroom's flimsy and overcrowded, with pin-tucked cushions on chairs standing a careful inch away from the walls. There's no room for ghosts here, no wooden shutters fastened open with spidery vines or thatched roof filled with impish toyol spirits. The jungle's been cut back too, and the massy trunks left outside are snaked with strangler figs. Trees with stranglers on them die, given enough time. They rot away inside, crumble so quietly you never even know.

Dilip taps at the door. "Shalini, are you decent?" – as though I've ever been anything else – and hefts the bags in.

"There," he wheezes, and sinks into one of the chairs. He closes his eyes and for a second we sit together, listening to the vanilla hum of the air conditioning.

"This'll be good for us." He keeps his eyes shut, as though he's hoping to open them on brighter, better things than we've managed so far. "A fresh start, eh? A few days by ourselves."

Without opening his eyes he reaches out and crumples my fingers into the hollow of his palm. He's taken his ring and watch off and the strips of skin beneath are pale as breath on a window. Underneath everything, in all his soft, hidden places where the words run out, I can still feel the pulse of his heart.

Perhaps there are some toyols left in this house making mischief at the edges of things after all, because our evening doesn't go as planned. The hotel dining room turns out to be the old kitchen, skinned over with eggshell paint and chandeliers. We all look lumpish and cream-fed in that glare, squeezed into mothball suits and satin dresses tight as someone else's skin.

"Sir, madam, what can I get you tonight?" It's Adelia again, with a sealed-up smile you couldn't get a fingernail under. There's a warmth in Dilip after he sees her, a cindery concentration to the way he talks. For the rest of the evening we haul our conversation along, and I learn her shape by the way he looks away.

She brings us kueh lapis for dessert and at the first taste of the pandan syrup I can feel Elsie elbowing her way back into things. She used to grow pandan here by the kitchen, where the squawking orioles pecked through my mother's dug-up flowerbed. Elsie knows all about what isn't there, so it's hardly a surprise that she's peeking out now from the crook of Adelia's elbow and the turn of her lovely heel.

The room's noisy now and the air tastes used-up, but I order a brandy and watch the dampness on Dilip's neck. Somewhere beneath the pandan and his hot, toasty savour, I can smell pomade in a birds-nest of hair.

In the bedroom he closes his eyes, lumbering into me with the heaves of someone giving it his best effort. He's turned the light off too, as if to make doubly sure, and from somewhere out of this gigantic darkness Elsie shrugs. She looks at me, tinkers with the oiled tangles of her hair. You got yourself into this, she says.

Elsie always was practical, even before she became this smooth ghost with a know-it-all smile. She would sit on the verandah combing her hair, while I padded about the house cradling my quarrels like a snake mouthing eggs. My father stretched and stretched between us, thin as chewed bubble-gum and just as appetising.

The ring he chose for her was a clot of opals that stuck tight below her knuckle. My mother's had been a loose hoop of diamonds that she'd kept slipping off to wipe a dish or type a letter or spend a night with her own Mr-Working-Late. No wonder he sized Elsie's a notch too small.

And as for Elsie, she only took hers off once. She left it on the dressing table one morning while she bathed. Just an ordinary morning, muddled and grey and full of the din of junglefowl after rain. Nothing portentous about that, Elsie, about a sulking thirteen-year-old creeping into your room, about a sky the colour of blankets and your ring sitting there for all the world like you thought it belonged. *Like pandan in a flowerbed?* she asks me now, from under the lurching bed. *Like a pontianak, Shalini, crossing her legs on the Ampang Line?*

Someone once told me that opals don't last, that their colour's just a trick of the rock. If you drop them in water – if you fling them, for example, into a flooded mineshaft filled with koi that never brought anyone any luck at all – then they fade. They dissolve till there's nothing left at all but your own nodding reflection and your dripping strands of hair.

When Dilip finally beaches himself in the bed's cotton shallows I sit up and look out of the window. The pontianaks outside are quiet now – what do they have to worry about, after all? – and the grass they're hiding in is drenched, sodden and secret as a peach beneath its skin.

By morning, the sky's whipped with mares-tail clouds and the hills are slick with heat. Nothing moves in the gardens except for a clump of curling touch-me-nots and one of the kitchen-cats shaking dew off its scabby paws. Dilip takes us out for an early walk; he likes to get at the day before it's ragged.

"Used to be mining country, up here." He prods at a springing hedge of bougainvillea and stands with his legs apart, breathing great nosefuls of air.

"Yes," I say politely. He's brought us up to the edge of the garden at a parade-ground clip and the earth feels loose and wet beneath my shoes. "The mines flooded, though," I tell him. "There were ponds left everywhere."

"Ponds?" He gives a hearty laugh, so blunt it couldn't possibly hurt. "The pits would've been blocked up, Shalini, not turned into ponds." He smacks a kiss on my cheekbone. Affectionate, the way you'd slap a horse.

"There *were*," I insist, and to my surprise there are tears at the back of it. Middle-aged, choky tears; the type to push in where they're not wanted, to drizzle on tubs of Chinese pomade and empty dressing tables.

"Don't get upset, Shalini." Dilip sounds exhausted, as though he'd like to snort through that fine nose and slip back into Miss Working-Late's arms. But he's a decent sort of fellow, ready to make allowances for the time of the month or last night's brandy. "Look, why don't you have the morning to yourself, eh?" he suggests. "Bit of down-time."

He gives my shoulder a friendly squeeze and strides away over the boggy grass. The wind's dropped since we came out, and a brassy light slaps the leaves awake. A few raindrops begin to fall, wetting the bougainvillea flowers till they're frail as Elsie's nightgowns. We're all in this together, me and the flowers and the waxy leaves, all of us wilting as my husband walks away.

We'd come right to the edge of the grounds, and it takes him a few minutes to reach the house. Halfway there he pauses and turns away, heading past the old kitchen. Rain comes down in heavy drops thick as honey, and Dilip's treading through flowerbeds he'll never know were there. Past the orioles, long dead and angry about it, past the teak trees pulled out like missing teeth, and then he's almost out of sight.

The hotel's slanting roof looks precarious from here, as though one day all that glass might coil a little tighter and swallow everything up. I can see two huge bins of laundry stacked under the wall where my bedroom used to be and Adelia stands next to them. She's pulling sheets out and stuffing them into a plastic laundry sack.

Dilip stops when he sees her, standing there with the linen in her arms like strings of pondweed. She bobs her head at him in a long, slow nod and I close my eyes. I hear leaves pattering about, cartwheeling away like kisses being blown.

When I open my eyes again, Dilip's still here; he's closing the door behind Adelia in a gentleman-like manner. Through the gap I can see her clipping down the passage, her arms full of sleep-stained linen and her skirt switching about her polished knees. Miss Working-Early. And then the door shuts and Dilip's still there. He's tiny from this distance, small and manageable and blameless as milk. Just like I thought I always wanted.

A rising wind begins to lick across the valley, bringing the raw-silk rip of tearing leaves. In between the gusts of rain, I can hear the pontianaks mutter and feel them press their cold, unloved sides against mine. I turn my back on the lot of them and walk a few steps away, where a spine of rock lifts under peppery tufts of grass. On the other side the lawn dwindles into a scrubby jungle scattered with trees. They're all twisted, warped by strangler figs into great swollen coils. A slop of water glimmers beneath in the distance, skimmed with algae and greying leaves.

Elsie once told me the monsoon started early here, that she could hear the wind in the stopped-up sockets of the mines. She said the water tasted of tin and the wells were crammed with ghosts. She said there was a lot I didn't see, hidden under the skin. She said a wife was always the last to know.

My hands are cold and I shove them deep into my pockets. It's last year's skirt, it's an inch too tight and my ring rips the waistband slightly. It's the kind of tear I won't get around to mending, the kind that will grow bigger and bigger over the next few years till it's large enough to swallow Miss Working-Late and Miss Working-Early and Miss Never-Worked-At-All. And then one unremarkable afternoon the whole thing will tear in two and I'll be sitting there on the Ampang Line, crossing and re-crossing my legs at businessmen going home.

Subjunctive Moods

"In Russia, you would be adorable." Katya pronounces the word carefully. Her English is halting, but she's mastered the subjunctive. *Were, would be; if everything were different.* She's good at missed opportunities.

When Katya says this to me I'm thirteen years old and she's staying with us on school exchange. She's fifteen and Russian, a combination which seems to me to create an immense and glamorous distance between us. I suspect they grow up earlier in Russia anyway; my brother Philip doesn't have this confidence she wears like a coat. His class went to Moscow for two weeks last year, and he came back saying it was just like the Cold War.

"There's concrete everywhere, Sara," he told me. "And fleas in the classroom."

Photos from their trip are still pinned to the school noticeboard. "Russia '94: School Exchange" – Philip with his arms wide in a crowd of shirtless boys. It doesn't look like the Cold War. The boys seem happy and unravelled somehow, with loose grins above bodies I've only ever seen in school uniform. I don't trust those smiles; I'm still at the stage where my crushes are fully clothed.

Most of the Russian students who've come to England this year are in the photos, but not Katya. She was there, Philip said, but she isn't really Russian. She was born somewhere else – she's Balkan, or Serbian, or maybe even Croatian. She's from somewhere I've only read about; somewhere with white Muslims and Orthodox Christians, with idols and pale-eyed women in the snow.

When Katya tells me I'm adorable we're in my mother's room with the curtains drawn. Piles of crumpled skirts and tops are puddled at our feet. We're playing dress-up, or something like it; I haven't yet realised that we're trying on different skins. Katya pulls me in front of the mirror and tugs my skirt down.

"See, this. Like a woman –" She shapes the gesture with her hands and gives up, unable to find a word that encompasses my hips. "Comme une femme," she substitutes. "You are adorable, in Russia."

She steps into a ruffled skirt from my mother's wardrobe and stands very still, judging herself. When she's seen enough she draws her mouth down in a hard, grown-up way and pinches at the fit around her waist. She's already thin, but pinned into someone else's clothes she looks even less substantial. More foreign, more slippery. As though she could turn up anywhere.

At school, Katya sits in my brother's Russian classes. I picture her, unmoving, staring out of the window at the frozen hockey fields. The playground floods every winter, leaving behind a litter of sticks and tiny, dead-eyed fish. In a year's time I'll begin learning Russian too, sitting at those desks and finding words hidden under my tongue. Words for fish, for flood, for concrete and the span of my hips. If everything were different.

Between classes, Amanda plants herself in front of our shared locker. Amanda's small and sinewy, like a sleek little forest animal. She's holding her breath, wrapping her ponytail over her mouth as though at any moment she might just choke.

"What's that smell?" Holly asks her obligingly, and Amanda looks at me. She doesn't do this for fun, that glance says. She's brimming with the same virtue as when she announces an extra hockey practice or additional swimming trials. These things are disagreeable, she implies in her sports prefect voice, but they're for our own good.

We've shared a locker all year, after Mrs Strickland assigned us partners. She read them out at the first assembly, to the sound of groans or squeals or a spreading pool of silence.

"Bad luck, Amanda," Holly said into that silence and Mrs Strickland coughed, resettled her guilty glasses. Holly's sharing with a girl called Fliss, both of them blonde and perfectly matched, the kind who belong in pairs. Sometimes I catch Amanda watching them with a look I've felt from the inside. I can't put it into words, that look. I would need Katya to translate.

Occasionally Amanda slips things through the vent in my locker. A stick of deodorant, a chewed apple core, a picture of fat Chinese children exercising. Perhaps these things are gifts, of a sort, or revenge. Perhaps I don't have a word for what they are.

The girl I'd like to share a locker with would be called Jill. Jill would gaze out of the window in double maths; she would wait for me at the bus stop and have a beautiful singing voice and ask me for help with her differential calculus. But Jill doesn't exist. Jill is the friend I'd like to have, given the option. If things were different, says Katya. If I were to have friends. Bad luck, Sara.

Each night Katya offers to help with my homework. Maths and physics, that's what she's good at, in a way that suggests she's learnt them already. In Russian, or Serbian, perhaps, in flea-ridden classrooms with shirtless boys.

"You add here, and here," she says, pointing. We're learning spheres: volume, radius, diameter, as though our adult world will be full of these precise, spiky little calculations. Next to the biggest, bulgiest sphere, Holly's scribbled a single word: "Sara". Holly, who sits next to me yawning her way through maths lessons, who droops her eyelashes and draws snake tattoos on her wrist, who will probably fail her exams and it won't matter a bit, whatever Mrs Strickland says.

Katya licks her finger and turns that page over quickly. She has a decisive air, as though she's about to say something for my own good.

"Sara," she says, and touches my hand. "Do you want to – to reduce?"

I don't know what she means at first. Subtraction, or simplification? We've learnt this recently: a way to make sense of thorny equations, to chop our problems into bite-size chunks. She explains energetically – oh, you mean *dieting*, Katya, we say *I'm on a diet* – and twists her hands as she talks. She has bony wrists, and they move in perfect spheres.

Her friends do it, back home, she tells me. Not vomiting – to regurgitate, we have to look that one up too – but just dieting. "Always careful, Sara," she insists.

They strip down to their underwear, she says, and compare ribs and hip bones in the school bathrooms. I wonder what they see, all those naked girls stranded on a wet concrete floor like fish after a flood. They're reducing; they're simplifying, shrinking to a point where they might just disappear. Where they might turn up anywhere. Katya smiles at me.

"You hide your food, Sara," she says. "In a napkin, or – wait." She vanishes into her bedroom, comes out again with a wispy blue scarf. "You knot on your neck – see?" She ties it for me. "And then, here, you put food from your plate into it. Hiding."

She turns me towards the mirror, giving the scarf a final tweak. I look raffish in it, rather daring and jaunty. Like a girl who scribbles on books, who belongs in pairs.

"But," I object, just once. "You said before… you said in Russia big hips were – were pretty."

Katya shrugs. She draws her mouth down and steps to one side, out of the mirror's reach. "Adorable. It isn't the same."

She says it kindly. Simplification: to rid of extraneous terms.

At dinner I slip a forkful of lamb quietly into the scarf. My mother doesn't notice; her eyes are on her plate and she's eating fast. At any moment the phone might ring, she'll be thinking, and she'll have to go back to work. I think Philip sees me, but he doesn't say anything. We're on the same side in a way that's hard to define, a slippery sort of way where it might turn out that he doesn't even know it. To him, I'm like Jill. I'm like Amanda's secret gifts and those Russian girls on the wet concrete floor. I don't need to be explained.

After dinner Katya helps me unknot the scarf. I tip it out into the bin while Philip clatters the dishes, and she brushes it clean.

"There," she says. "It is easy?"

There's a spiky calculation in the perfect sphere of my stomach: twelve hours until breakfast. Katya puts her arm around me and giggles. She kisses my cheek, and in my head I see a bathroom in Moscow with a hundred reflected Saras being kissed by a hundred mirrored Katyas. I give those Russian Saras – those Svetlanas – jutting hip bones. I give them perfect skin and headscarves bright red against the snow and best friends named Jelena with beautiful singing voices.

The next morning Katya calls me from her bedroom. We're all in a rush; Philip has a chemistry test and wants my mother to drop him off early. He likes to be well prepared, to beat all those boys with their loose-jawed grins and deceptively skinny shoulders. It's his version of adulthood, of the Weetabix in my scarf.

"Here, Sara." Katya's wearing her Russian school uniform. All the exchange students do, and their fluttering yellow ribbons and brave blue jumpers give them a finished air, as though school is just a dress-up game. Katya doesn't talk to the others much, the ones in Philip's photographs. When she's around them she reduces herself to a dot, somewhere always behind the camera. To a trick of the light.

"Take these," she tells me, holding out a gift-wrapped package. "They're – good. Good chance." *Lucky*, we look up in her dictionary. Katya's English seems to be getting worse, or perhaps it's a word she's never needed. Inside the packet there's a handful of aluminium stars, the kind you thread a piece of cotton to and hang in windows. They're tumbled together with lavender soap and some supermarket chocolate. She must have been told to bring host gifts, like Philip was, but these are all the wrong things. She knows better, now, than she did when she packed. Katya moves on, I think. She leaves things behind.

"Take them, Sara. To give you – luck." She keeps hold of my hands and mumbles the last word, as though testing out its flavour. She isn't sure; it doesn't suit her hard mouth and bony wrists. She's taking a risk, I know. Hoping I won't rub off.

"I heard you liked PE today, Sara," Amanda sings out as I walk to our locker that afternoon. She isn't even in my PE class, but Holly is. Holly with her ballpoint tattoos and beautiful eyes, Holly who heard Mrs Bugloss tell me not to attempt the ropes.

"I don't want to spend an hour lifting heavy girls down from where you've got yourselves stuck," she said. "Sara, Beth – go to the balance beams instead." I tramped off with Beth, who never runs anywhere, and Elise with her lung problems and Grace who'd forgotten her sports kit. Beth's hip bumped against mine as we clambered on to the beams, and she looked away.

"Did you, Sara? Did you like it?" Holly's watching me, and Amanda is too, standing a little behind her. The corridor's quiet, full of that end-of-the-day limpness, and outside I can hear the younger children shrieking. Katya's stars are in my pocket, smooth and hard-edged, blank and to the point and no help at all.

"And how are you getting on with Katie?" Amanda asks.

There's a faint edge of irritation in her voice, a flicker of pity at the end. She'd rather I answered back, presented a smaller target. Covering so much ground isn't fair on her.

"Who's Katie?" I ask, and Holly bursts into giggles.

"Katie," she says. "Your exchange."

"Oh, Katya," I say, and blush. I sound like Mrs Strickland, insisting on using our full names. I didn't know Katya had a nickname.

"She's helping you diet, isn't she?" Amanda comes closer, putting her arm around my neck. To anyone else we'd look like friends. Perhaps we are. "Katie told Natacha it was so sad, seeing you like this. They're all so sorry for you."

Natacha's another of the exchange students, staying with Amanda's family. I know Natacha; she's in the middle of all of Philip's photographs, she has thick blonde hair and a grey school jumper lent by Amanda's besotted older brother, which she wears casually knotted around her waist. In that jumper she blends in; she can hide in plain sight. I feel queasy. My scarf is stained with food and hangs limp over my breasts. I wonder what the Russian for lonely is. I wonder if Katya knows the English.

Amanda turns back once as they walk away. Her eyes are wide and she's warning me off, but I don't know from what. They've left my locker covered with a construction paper sign saying I'm On A Diet, with a picture of bulging balloons and a spherical pink pig. It's drawn well; Holly hasn't been wasting her time in those maths lessons after all.

There's something inside the locker too, one of Amanda's gifts. It's yet another postcard of those fat Chinese girls exercising – and where did she get so many? Did Natacha bring them as host gifts, like Katya's stars? – but Amanda's scribbled over this one with a thick black pen.

She's only left a single chink of flesh, a pale slice of arm that's been shrunk to a dot. I rip the paper sign down, fold it up with the postcard and Katya's star, and slot the whole package through the vent in Amanda's locker. It's thank-you, in a way, or perhaps it's revenge. It's an assassination attempt, or maybe a surrender treaty. It's an event on the edge of happening.

When I've been home an hour I hear Katya and Philip come in, but I don't answer her knock. I brush out the scarf, re-tie it and slip my dinner into it again under cover of Philip forking up potatoes. I leave the table before dessert, and later that evening I ask my mother if Katya can go to another family for the rest of her stay.

They're supposed to move on, I explain, Mrs Strickland said we had to organise it. Philip gives me a tiny nod, just once, like a semaphore from somewhere behind his physics book. Mum shakes her head in confusion. Nobody told me, she says, and then later – to herself – I thought you all were friends.

A few days later Philip comes top in his physics test and I see Katya for the first time since Mum persuaded Mrs Strickland to find her another host family. She's far away, on the other side of the frozen hockey fields with Natacha, and for a moment I think it might not be her at all. When they come closer I see Katya wears a grey jumper around her waist too now. They have matching ballpoint tattoos on their wrists, and she no longer looks like it's all just a dress-up game.

Lucky Katya – good chance. *Vezuchiy*. It turns out there was a word for it all along.

When I'm older I see Katya again. By now the news coming out of Eastern Europe is bad; places are under siege and people are disappearing. Katya would have known what to do, I think, and she turns up where I least expect it. She's in the flash of a ruffled skirt that I see through the bus window. She's in Mum's drawn-down smile, or Mrs Strickland's careful pauses in assembly. She's in a ponytail, a bony wrist waving from a taxi, a chink of skin where a passing cyclist rolls up his sleeve. I see her on the news, too, being herded into a Red Cross evacuation centre or fixing a gun. She's good at disguise, I know. She could slip out of the country, be anywhere she wanted.

By now I have my own bony wrists, and I'm about to leave school. I share a locker with Fliss, who's turned out to have a beautiful singing voice. I see Katya for a year or two, then forget. She's somewhere else, with Jill and Natacha. They're holding aluminium stars and dictionaries on the roof of a Cold War building, they're all in headscarves and all of them are on the run.

Aunty

It wasn't till after we burnt her that Leila began to cause trouble. It started early, while Gupta's crematorium smell was still tweaking our lungs and Leila was sifting in the ice-cream tub on Mohini's windowsill.

While she was alive, Leila had soothed our nightmares. She'd kissed our foreheads; she'd turned on the bathroom light to scare away the pontianaks; she'd bandaged our knees and helped with our sums. But now that she was dead, all that changed. Now, she was knotting the brothers' ties into tangles instead; she was tossing the sisters' jewellery into the talcum powder box and winding the clocks backwards each night. Our dreams stretched thin as rice-paper as we overslept and the cook swore among his saucepans while our breakfast went cold.

"Wah! She's in a plastic tub only? You need glass, Mohini-child. That will fix her."

Aunty Bibi's long, quivering nose had smelled trouble all the way from next door. She arrived three days after the funeral, muttering Cantonese curses and stumping her way over the calla lilies. She dropped a box of laddoo on the kitchen table, shooed the pontianaks away from the door with such vigour that they soured the milk, then plumped into a dining chair to eat the cook's congealed nasi lemak. Bibi had cremated two husbands and stoppered them up in vases on her polished windowsills. She knew how to keep ghosts in line.

"We're getting an urn soon, Bibi-Aunty. This was all we had."

Mohini hadn't stopped crying since the funeral. She slept, she bathed, she scolded the younger children and licked kaya off her butter-knife all behind a glassy fall of tears. Ali-Driver and Ali-Hawker both came by to comfort her, one after another, and she pressed damp, luminous kisses into the creases of their necks. When she'd stripped the chauffeur's cap from one and the satay sticks from the other, she led each boy into her bedroom and loosed those civet-cat screams she'd learnt from Meg Ryan at the Shaw Palace. We hoped one of these scuffles would clear the air, but after a few hours the liquid murmur returned and Mohini brought out a boy sodden and salty as a mermaid with all the coconut oil sobbed out of his hair.

Bibi made her disapproval clear. She disliked the crumpled neckties, the dirty butter-knives and the way the younger children's dressing gowns scampered empty through the halls when our backs were turned.

"Well." She swallowed the last chilli from the nasi lemak and coughed – a glorious, palate-scouring snort – that made all the plates upend themselves and quiver in disgust. Bibi muttered something in Cantonese.

"Too delicate for snot, eh, Leila?"

Leila had been fastidious even before she was a ghost. At the height of the flu her plump fingers had darted under her nose to catch any drips before they swung free. She'd never yawned or belched, and when she'd had hiccups she'd retreated to her room for two days and lived on stale fruitcake until they subsided.

"She'll make trouble, that one. You lock her up, Mohini-child."

And with that, Bibi kissed us all and sailed away through the lilies, leaving shipwreck behind her. That night there were footsteps in the attic and splashing in the bone-dry sinks. Leila's invisible fingers tugged our pillows away, tied birdseed to the kitchen-cats' tails and squeezed six lemons into her almirah to kill the silverfish that were eating her scarves.

And then it was a moist, fog-sopped morning and Mohini was screaming from her tiny bedroom. She slept in a dim little place, smelling of the Alis' loincloths mingled with her cotton underwear in a soup of warmth and curling hair.

"Mohini! Child, open the shutters."

Bibi danced in a panic under the window, banging on the crumbling bricks. That nose of hers had been on the alert all night, much to the terror of the pontianaks scrambling in and out of her storm-drains to soak their two-clawed feet. She'd smelled the dust from Leila's footsteps and the cats' hissing rage, but it was the lemons that had her up at dawn. Their smell had reached right into her house and under her mosquito net, it had dragged her from her dreams and brought her through the dripping grass to hear Mohini's first scream.

"Mohini! Open up!"

One of the shutters crawled open to show a slice of bare throat and shoulders.

"My clothes are gone, Bibi-Aunty. Leila's cut them."

And she had. One of the sisters reported that Mohini's miniskirts hung like spinach-leaves from the hallway fan. A brother found the remains of her T-shirts soaking among the swamp weed and Mohini topped it all off by mournfully handing her underwear out through the window, to show us how every opening had been sewn shut with Leila's tiny, perfect stitches.

"Mohini, child, you can't stay like that." Bibi was practical, and worried about chills. "Wear Leila's clothes from the almirah. Just for today."

Mohini looked doubtful. Leila had spent hours tailoring those clothes into the shape she'd yearned for, nipping in where she didn't nip and tucking out where she'd never tucked. She'd hemmed jackets and pinned trousers, had peeled her tights off and darned them every evening in the hope they'd somehow transform her thighs. Each of us, creeping into Leila's almirah for games of hide-and-seek, had breathed in camphor and the sadness of clothes that had never quite fit. Now, the sisters helped Mohini pull the doors open and an old Huntley & Palmers tin rattled off the shelf to spill a mouthful of pins onto her toes.

"Leila-Aunty, it's your own fault," Mohini argued plaintively, and she began to browse through the clanking wire hangers.

When she came out in Leila's second-best yellow dress, in the tight-seamed stockings and white sash, she walked more slowly than before. It suited her, we agreed together, the way Leila's dress packed her into shape. Her miniskirts had left her inclined to flightiness and had set the sisters a bad example.

"There, child." Bibi was still standing on the flowerbed, arms and legs akimbo in case Leila was planning any more mischief. She clambered out and whisked some lint from Mohini's shoulder. "You're decent again."

But Mohini was more than just decent. Leila's skirt wrapped itself around her legs all day and shrank her steps. The sash pinched however she tied it, and when Ali-Driver came by she had to send him away because neither of them could understand how to loosen Leila's petticoat hooks.

And to make matters worse, Aunty Bibi had been right about the urn. The plastic ice-cream tub we'd carried in four days ago had begun to leak tiny flakes of ash. Leila drifted through the air, getting into the spices and under our tongues until Mohini's hair turned a premature, sprinkled grey and everything tasted of cinders. We closed the shutters to stop Leila from getting out and giving the swamp-ghosts ideas, and stifled in the muddy gloom.

"Mohini-Aunty, look at our sums, please." The younger children clung to Mohini's legs, wadding themselves against yellow silk thighs they thought they remembered.

She didn't understand sums, she argued, slapping them away with an older-sister glare. But in the midday twilight the younger children became panicky, filled with a frail kind of love that left them clawing at her knees and tugging her hair out of its ponytail.

"Mohini-Aunty, the sums!"

One of them pulled at the pocket of her yellow skirt, ripping it and setting a tiny waterfall of Leila's belongings tumbling free. A worn-down pencil, a jumble of hairgrips and three cancelled train tickets.

"What's that?" Mohini plucked the tickets back, held them up to her eyes. The blurred light was giving her a squint and the same furrowed brow Leila had when the lamp-wicks needed trimming.

"They're all to the airport," she said, and frowned. "When did she go there?"

We looked at each other, the brothers and the sisters swapping glances that sidled round the edges of the room. In the corner a mosquito coil glowed bright red, and one of the brothers stubbed it out.

"She didn't go, Mohini-Aunty," one of us said. "She didn't catch the trains."

"And I'm not an aunty!" The spinning fan had tangled Mohini's hair into flossy hanks, and the older sisters quietly pinned them back with Leila's hairgrips. "What happened to her?"

It was a brother, or perhaps a sister, who answered first.

"The mosquitoes, Aunty. When you were away at school, remember? The malaria."

"I have a ticket!"

Leila planted her hands on her hips, spongy and stocking-less under her dress. She'd joined the crowd outside the shabby train station at dawn in her slippers and third-best apron, carrying whatever she'd grabbed from the house as we slept. A mop, a packet of flour and the younger children's arithmetic homework juggled for space in her wicker basket.

"Madam, it's quarantine. If you carry out the malaria, then what?" The guard was young and fresh as scrubbed bamboo cane, with his rifle stick-straight against the blackened, buzzing sky.

"Pah!" Leila snapped, dismissing malaria and quarantine alike with a snap of her fingers. She pushed him aside with her mop, leaving a splodge of wet soap to take the curl from his hair and the starch from his jacket. A stiff yellow banner had been pasted over the ticket office in the middle of the night and the tracks lounged shimmering and deserted except for a few bony dogs. Like Leila, everyone had booked their tickets weeks before and a crowd flocked along the road with little queasy cries like gulls in a storm. Businessmen carried bags and suitcases, flower sellers balanced feathery sheaves of hibiscus petals on their heads and ayahs bundled children under their arms like chickens trussed for market. The sunlight was filmy, filtering through an immense cloud of mosquitoes that boiled above the patient hills.

Three miles away, that cloud of mosquitoes was rising in a bubbling funnel from a fish-pond in our garden. The brothers, being the best at nature study, had been in charge this time. They'd spent weeks coaxing mosquitoes to the pond, ever since we'd found Leila's ticket in her shapeless handbag. They'd stretched their bare legs out by the water every evening to tempt mosquitoes grown hungry or sly, and every morning they'd rescued larvae from puddles that could dry up in the noontime sun. The sisters helped, too, covering the pool in a mat of swamp weed and snatching out any koi that put up its golden, gappy lips through the twisting stems.

Now, we sat cross-legged on the grass among fish bones delicate as ivory combs. A sister leant over and dabbled her fingers, stirring more mosquitoes to join the cloud that would cover the town for a week. It would smother the sun and dim the street lamps until three children died of malaria and one of fright, until the flower sellers dropped their bundles to blossom by the roadside, until Leila missed her train and returned home just in time to correct our sums.

"But… the other tickets?" Mohini's tears had dried by now, leaving her cheeks cracked and pitted. We rubbed at her temples, soothing her. "What happened?"

She stayed quite still while we told her, while we pinned her hair and straightened her sash. The second time, we explained, Ali-Hawker had promised Leila she could borrow his tricycle to get to the station. But a sister made sure the garden gate was swinging open as Ali brought the tricycle, tempting him into a shortcut through the hedges and into a draught of scented air spilling from Mohini's open window. That scent made him drop the handlebars, leave the wheels spinning among anthills and buddleias while he climbed in with a shaking need. Half an hour later his tricycle collapsed under Leila on the road, its hinges flying apart with the shock of Ali's first kiss and his discovery of what lay under the flightiness of Mohini's miniskirts.

The final time Leila locked herself in the attic by mistake after a brother oiled the latch that had, in any case, been sticking for too long. She spent a night there with the civet-cats, peering out between strands of the attap roof while she caught the chill that would eventually kill her. The attic, we said, was strung with spiders in their silky webs, and littered with the kiss-curls of dried-up centipedes. It was a place where things ended up; everything from toys to burnt saucepans, from the brothers' first wet dreams to the sisters' peaceable nightmares, from aunties to civet-cats.

Now, some things are different. We've shared the rest of Leila's clothes out, the ones that wouldn't fit Mohini however she stitched. The jackets have been turned into dressing gowns, to replace the ones that still scamper shamefacedly in cupboards where they think nobody will notice. The scarves have gone to the brothers, in place of the neckties still knotted in tricky tangles about the door handles. We gave Aunty Bibi a skirt in return for one of her stoppered vases, and Leila now lives bottled up in glass on a stand of polished jambu wood.

And we wait.

We're decked out in scarves that smell of camphor and shirts that don't quite fit. We oversleep each morning, we turn our backs on the darkened corridors and tug our pillows straight and send the cook home to make nasi lemak for his own children. Ali-Hawker and Ali-Driver don't visit any more and Mohini's nose has grown long and troublesome as Leila's. Every night she darns her stockings in Leila's room, padding about barefoot over rusty pins and squeezed-out lemon peel. And we sit down in the oil-lamp blackness of the attic to play mah-jongg with the pontianaks, and we listen to those pulpy footsteps and we wait for our aunty to decide to leave.

Watermelon Seeds

Peony has whiskers; she has a pointy face and a tail made out of blue raffia; she's messing about in boats and dabbling-up-tails-all, and I am in love.

"You have to say 'Blow spring-cleaning!' now, Anjali," she insists, and jumps with a splash of patent-leather shoes right into the tricky, rippling flood that swirls down the gutter between our houses. The monsoon is coming, and the water will soon be ankle-deep and silted up with rotting fruit. But Peony and I don't care because by then we'll be inside, watching a Cantonese soap opera on her drawing-room television and eating fried watermelon seeds. She'll crack one open between her teeth and I'll taste it a split-second before she swallows, because Peony and I are two-together, like dots on a domino, and everything we feel is the same.

We were given our parts for the school play today; it was chatter-and-elbows in front of the noticeboard; it was congratulations waved off – *so much fuss, lah! all talk-talk* – and tears in the padang outside the school gate. I'm an understudy for Mole, but Peony, oh, Peony is going to be Ratty, and how could anyone not be in love? Mr and Mrs Wong will come to watch her in the dark school gym with the fans spinning high up in the rafters where you can only reach if you climb one-two feet-together up a plaited rope in your gym skirt. They will sit on the folding metal chairs and the spotlights will glint off their spectacles and mosquitoes will bite at their ankles, and none of this will matter because their daughter is Ratty in a river of light on stage, and this is where it all begins.

"Prompt me again, Anjali!" She reaches out for my hand and tugs me into the water too. My hands fold warm into hers and my feet bump up against her toes, and for a moment our faces float frail as ghosts somewhere below the water. And then she kicks up a giant spray, a fan of rainbow drops that soaks my dress and leaves her slumped solid and giggling against me.

"I won't play!" But I will, of course, and she pulls me up on the mud-splashed gutter to dangle my feet next to hers in the stream.

"Blow spring-cleaning…?" I offer tentatively. Her face splits into a wide, wide smile as she sails into her lines, and I think my heart breaks, just a little bit, because now Peony is Ratty again. This is our last day before the holidays and I want to save every little bit of it, to squeeze it up tight in my hands.

"Come and watch TV with me, Anjali," she says as she steps toe-heel out of her shoes on the shallow steps of the Wong's verandah. A stone lion guards the door, and I stroke its face, already blurred from years of our hugs. The hall behind it smells of silence, of lilies and rosewater and cool polished wood, and Peony disappears down it like a breath against the wind. Next door, my own quiet house reeks of coconut oil and turmeric. *Such a Tamil smell*, Mrs Wong said once when she thought we were upstairs, and for months after that Peony and I mouthed *Tamil smell* across the classroom to each other when we got our homework wrong.

"I have to pack first," I call to the fluttering lace of her dress. A breeze is coming down from the jungle and everything is alive with it. Along the padang the casuarina leaves are rustling and the soft petals of hibiscus are being slowly shredded. All through Kuala Lipis hair ribbons will be whipping and sarongs will be blowing, and everyone will know the monsoon is on its way from the polished pewter sky.

Peony turns at the end of the hall and calls back something rude in Cantonese. She's taught me a little and I know that these are bad words; grown-up words to reach into the future and pull the years and everything that waits in them tumbling down like a stack of dominoes onto her tangled black head. But then a silver curtain of rain sweeps down from the road and her skirt flutters in the dark of the hall and Peony is gone.

"Here, sir-madam. Colonial House." The driver glances back at us, glued tight as snails on the lumpish leather seats. His hair leaves a coconut oil smear on the back of his seat.

"Already we paid, so no money now, okay, lah?" My mother grabs at the back of his seat, smearing the hair-oil over her fingers (Tchee! So dirty!), and levers herself up from her mushroom of skirts and travelling rugs.

"Hello! Hello!" my father calls. "Come and help us unload." He slaps at his arms in a bluff and hearty way I don't recognise, as though somewhere on the journey someone has slipped a different Appa into our car. The verandah gate opens and a bearded fleet of uncles and uncles-by-marriage begin to steam up like full-bellied sailing ships.

"Out you get, little Anjali, lock, stock and barrel." The uncles are like this, I remember, full of mysterious phrases with the sense sucked out of them. Barrels mean rum, I think, and pirates and fifteen men on a dead man's chest. *Tamil-smell uncles*, I whisper, but Peony is miles away back home with the watermelon seeds and the tumbling monsoons and nobody hears me. I slide down flat in my seat until my bare knees joggle the seat in front, and I listen to an uncle drop our bags plump-plump on the ground.

"Come on, Anjali!"

Behind that verandah is my grandfather's house, and behind that are the courtyards. They stretch out like a rope of caves, each of them darker than the next and filled with banyan trees and swamps and bricked-up wells. The window shutters are open upstairs and I can see the faces of my cousins, crammed in like mice in a nest. Each year they arrive before us, stepping lordly off the plane from England instead of being lock-stock-barrelled out of a station taxi. They leave a sort of silt wherever they go – hair-ties and pencil shavings and faded perfume – and for the next two weeks I will pick my way through this in the spaces that are left.

A door slams inside, and then the aunties troop kajal-eyed out onto the verandah, bulging from their saris and warm as cats from an afternoon nap. Amma begins to shuffle from her seat, muttering the complaints she's been saving in her throat for their loving ears, and I follow all alone like a single dot on a domino.

"Girls, take Anjali with you today. I'm sure she knows some new games." My cousins and I swap silent, muttering glances over our breakfast plates. *How-can-**she**-know-anything*, and *Leave-me-alone*, and underneath all that a sort of awkward *it's not your fault though*, like bumping elbows with a friend in the dark.

"If she wants to, Mummy." Priya is the oldest girl-cousin; she's fifteen and poised forever between the children and the kajal-aunties. I wonder if she likes this, or if she's too old for all this "liking-disliking", as my mother would say, and is therefore truly grown-up. Priya has a lovely faint smile, and a whitish face like ivory gone yellow; her voice is smooth and English and everything she says is the exact opposite of what she means.

I stare down at my Weetabix and don't say anything. There's a spoonful of Nutella on top, dolloped there by one of the aunties who doesn't know that Nutella is only for treats. I've been saving it for the final mouthful, but now

Priya's words are hanging in the air, and everything is melting into plain brown mush. Anjali, don't be such a baby, someone will say in a moment, and then the Weetabix will stick in my throat and Nutella will never be a treat again.

"She can come with me," Rahul says suddenly, and I look up in surprise. Rahul is thirteen and right in the middle of the boy-cousins. He has eyelashes like splashes of ink and slabbed front teeth too big for his mouth, and I want both those things too, with a kind of fierce and determined itch. Peony likes him, though she's only ever seen photographs, and begs me to tell her about him every year. She said once in Truth-or-Dare that she would marry him when she grew up, and I refused to play any more until she took it back.

"If you like," I mutter into my bowl, and swirl the milk around until Amma scolds and snatches it away, Nutella and Weetabix and baby-and-all.

"Are you going to play cricket?" I ask.

Rahul and the boy-cousins have stamped a pitch into the biggest courtyard, and out there they take turns to be heroes: Viv Richards and Peter Willey and others whose names I don't even know. I don't get to be a hero though, only a small and silly Anjali trailing after missed catches while jackfruit blossom drops on her head. I whisper one of Peony's rude words under my breath, and Rahul peers at me.

"No, I'm going to show you something. Come on, Anjali."

He takes me through the courtyards to the furthest corner, where durian trees mass together and banyans choke the walls. It looks like the horror movies Peony and I love, a swampy tangle where sharp-nailed ghosts and bloodsucking pontianaks shriek at night. The windows to the back bedrooms are high above us, and tonight our grandparents will mumble there, safe in their mosquito-netted dreams. For now, though, the shutters droop open in the sun, half-hidden by slack jowls of bougainvillea. A banyan tree looms overhead, its branches swooping down to a dim cave speckled with shadows and the tiny smells of the naked earth.

I put my hands on my hips, where the waist of my new dress ties. It's my favourite – blue cotton with ruffles – and the feel of the satin sash makes me brave. "I don't see anything," I say.

Rahul doesn't answer, just squats down and starts to scoop out a shallow trench. He digs it criss-crossing, a glistening gutter of earth that doubles back just beyond my toes. I watch him, listening to the pontianaks hissing from the banyan roots, then Rahul sits back on his heels with a look of triumph.

"There!" He wipes his hands clean on a patch of moss. "It's going to be a house, Anjali. Don't you see?"

And suddenly, I do. When I crouch down next to Rahul the ditches turn into walls, and beyond them are halls and rooms and endless jewelled courtyards where nobody will ever leave me out of games again. The pontianaks can cry all they like, and the other cousins can burrow like mice, but this is mine – all mine – and inside here I choose how everything turns out.

Rahul's left a space for the front door and I slide my shoes off heel-toe before walking through. He's forgotten to draw steps, but I climb them anyway with my knees high, and I pat the empty place by the door where my stone lion will be. "Blow spring-cleaning," I mutter, and from somewhere my skirt flutters in a breeze and there's a silver scent of rain.

"Anjali! So dirty, your feet! Aiyoh, do you think I'm coming here to wash and slave for you?" Amma is upset or she wouldn't talk like that, like she does at home. When we're at my grandfather's house she tries to speak nicely-nicely, like the English aunties.

"It was my fault, Aunt Sajni. We were playing in the courtyards." Rahul's voice is smooth as pebbles underwater, and it soothes Amma. She nods her head one-two-three along with all the other kajal-aunties who loll on kitchen chairs sipping mango juice and watching us eat. Amma nestles back into the middle of them, and her bite melts down to a purr of complaint somewhere deep in her plump dark neck.

Rahul beckons me over to the sideboard, where he's heaping a plate full of the soft white mounds of idli. He squeezes them together so they bulge like bosoms – fleshy like Amma or the big girls at school – and I start to giggle.

When Priya takes one, his fingers brush against mine and a little smile slinks between us, like a silver firefly in the deep-green dining room.

After lunch, Rahul and I wander outside, stranded and small in the beating bronze air. Everything is silent, and even the cats lie exhausted and slit-eyed in puddles of tar-black shade. Upstairs the girl-cousins are lying down too, in their vests and knickers with their strange white bodies beached beneath the mosquito nets. Like slugs, I tell Rahul, and when he laughs it fizzes cold and clear in my head.

In the durian courtyard the trees look baked, crisp and curled tight in the heat. I've been telling Rahul about our play; about Anjali-the-Mole and Peony-the-Ratty; about the stone lion I've hugged every morning before school; about the monsoon and the watermelon seeds and how Peony and I will one day be actors under the clear yellow sun in California. I don't think he's listening, but then he remembers to walk up our invisible steps and pat our stone lion, and I forgive him.

"We need a guest room, Anjali," he tells me, and I immediately start to squabble with him, in a comforting sort of way that I know doesn't really matter. A guest room has to have flowers, I insist, and he offers to climb the banyan tree where orchids clump above our heads, but I refuse. He has to creep back to the house, I tell him, and steal some fresh-cut flowers from my grandmother's vases. He mustn't be seen, and he must double back to confuse his tracks and stay downwind of the aunties to avoid being captured. His eyes gleam as he listens and his teeth shine wet, and for one moment I'm two-together again, and it feels disloyal and lovely.

While Rahul's gone I draw in our steps and our stone lion. Its face is sharp and its eyes are crossed, all the better to look both ways with. The soil must be damp, because a pool collects under my feet as I draw and soon my feet are wet from the squelching mud and mosquitoes are swarming beneath the lion's fur.

It's dusk by the time Rahul comes back. The sun slants gold through the vines, and glosses off the banyan leaves in a sunset haze. A cricket gives a tinny little chirrup, but the noise cuts off with a stutter of alarm as Rahul pushes back.

He's brought flowers from every vase in the house and they drip cool on my fingers, smooth and waxy and smelling of rosewater.

"Flowers for you, Anjali!" he says, and comes to sit next to me with his back against the garden wall. His arm is damp against mine and I watch a mosquito land under his ear, on that thumb patch of bare salt skin. A red lump starts to swell, but he's fiddling with the flower stems and doesn't notice, so for one moment there's a tiny secret about him that belongs just to me.

"There!" He passes me the flowers, plaited into a twining bouquet, and asks, "Will Peony be our first guest?"

I'd forgotten all about the guest room and I swallow. The flowers are wilting from being plaited, and their colours have already faded a little in the dry night air. Rahul slaps at his ear and says "Mosquito bite!" in a tone of surprise, and my secret is gone.

"I don't want Peony here," I tell him, and the pontianaks and devils nod one-two-three and purr down in their throats. "She wants to…" and now it's almost too late, and then one breath later I take his hand and then it is too late. "She wants to *marry* you." There's a pause, a heartbeat where nothing moves. His face is a glow of ivory in the dusk, and his ink-splash eyelashes are blinking soft as a breath. And then he spins around, and the air is thick with tiger-striped shadows, with the choking smell of durian and the sound of Rahul laughing.

I push him away and he whoops with a metallic sort of jeer, bitter like teeth on tinfoil. "You're in love!"

He's found it out and the secret's too big to keep to himself. It bites at his lips and squeals for air and the next moment it's sent him running with a cackle right into the knot of cousins in the next courtyard. His feet scuff our fragile walls and his sandal-thumps echo down our hallways and rooms.

When he's gone, when it's quiet and all the normal day-coloured sounds have come shuffling back, I lean against the garden wall. I whisper rude words in Cantonese under my breath and with the very tip of one finger I make a little trench around me, just enough to keep out the tiniest pontianak and the slowest devil.

Back at school, Peony still has her raffia tail; she still has her whiskers and her pointy face; she's still messing-about-in-boats, and for her, everything is still the same.

I don't look at her during class, and when the bell goes I stay in the classroom until she leaves, looking back at me in bewilderment. I don't tell her anything. I don't talk about the durian courtyard, or the pontianaks or the way those chants of *Anjali's in love, Anjali's in love* braided themselves through my cousins' singsong games. I take somebody else as my partner for gym class, and we climb one-two so high up a plaited rope that I think I might never come down again. And later, I give up my role in the school play and tell the drama teacher that Amma refused to let me join.

The night of the performance, I sit on my bedroom floor with the light off and a mosquito coil glowing under the bed. I watch cockroaches scuttle along the doorframe and breathe in Tamil smell and whisper "Bother spring-cleaning" into the gloom. But perhaps I get the timing wrong, because over in the school hall Peony forgets her lines and cries in the chalk-and-paint wings of the gymnasium stage.

Peony and I will never speak again, except for brief words with their tails caught sharp between our teeth. She will move to Kuala Lumpur to study drama, and when my mother rings to tell me about this I will pretend to have heard already. By then I will be in England, and not long afterwards I will marry an Englishman with pale white skin and hair the colour of sand. Our children will be fair as ivory, and their teachers will call me Angie; our house will smell only of floral air-freshener and my husband will, in any case, dislike turmeric.

And then, on those short summer nights when the air feels like home, I will slide my slippers off heel-toe and creep downstairs. I will find a Cantonese film on the television, while my sandy husband sleeps off his Sunday-night stew and the children lie beached under the drape of blankets. The heroine will smile out at me from the dark, and I will taste the watermelon seeds between her teeth, but she will never be Peony, not ever, and by then I won't understand a single word she says.

So Long, So Long

I used to be a god.

For ten years he had written that in his diaries. Front cover, back cover, three lines down on an anonymous Tuesday in March. He'd scrawled it on grocery lists, on electricity bills and the mist of a fly-speckled shaving mirror. He'd traced it, light as a moth, on the shallow bones of Priya's sleeping back.

The year he'd turned six, every boy in his school had been given a copy of the *Ramayana* by a thrifty headmaster. Most of the books ended up in kitchen bins or propping up rickety beds, but not Arjun's. In a family crammed with older siblings, with hand-me-downs and leftovers, this book was the first thing that was one-hundred-per-cent only his. He'd learnt to read from it, he'd practised his spelling in it and he'd added up its page numbers until his head spun and he came top of the class in arithmetic.

Every afternoon, Harun had tormented Arjun on the walk home. Harun was top in sports, top in English, top in everything that mattered. He'd lain in wait for Arjun by the school gates each day, and then he would throw Arjun's schoolbag into the gutter and slap him with the toughened ends of palm fronds. Arjun would run sobbing into his house, consoling himself with laddoos snatched from the cook and a few greedy minutes alone with his book. His tears would dry as he read how Rama plunged into the fire, how the rakshasa demons flashed through the skies. He dreamt of becoming them, of slicing Harun in two with a kitchen knife or tearing him apart like Hanuman did with mountains. One afternoon Harun had given him a black eye, and Arjun, inspecting it in the mirror, had seen his face shiver. His skin had melted away to show glass-green bones and the face of a god. If only Harun had known.

"Arjun! Where are you? Why are you late?"

He sighed as his wife's voice floated up from the tiny kitchen. The ceiling fan whirred, stirring the soupy air into currents that flicked at the pages of his old diaries on the desk. *I used to be a god.*

Priya was standing by the kitchen stove when he came down, her bare feet flat as bread on the tiled floor. She was frowning at a mess of eggs in the pan and gnawing the insides of her cheeks. That motion always made him think of blood, of a richness welling into the secret hollows of her mouth, but the dutiful morning kiss she gave him was dry and papery. She was wearing cheap gold bracelets, too bright against the pale cotton of her sari. It was only after little Bala's accident that she'd started to wear those white mourning clothes, without saying a single word to Arjun. Priya – dry, papery Priya with her secret springs of blood – had turned out to have her own secrets.

"You should have come down earlier." Her voice was high, tearless but catching in her throat. "The maid hasn't arrived, the children need to go to school, and here I am cooking breakfast for you!"

"Priya. I'm sorry... I'm sorry, but you know." He went towards her, leant awkwardly across the counter and felt it jut into the flesh of his belly. "I have to go to work."

She slammed the pan down and glared at him.

"Go to work, yes! To stay as a junior surgeon all your life? To fail your exams again?" Her voice rose to a screech. "I should never have followed you here. You're useless – all belly, no balls, no man!"

She slapped his upper arm, a weak little smack like a kitten jabbing at a ball of wool. At one time he wouldn't have dreamt either of them could have hit the other. At one time.

"Priya, look, it isn't so bad. It's..." Last night he had told her that he had failed his qualifying exams for the second time. He would not be a consultant this year, would probably not be retained at the hospital next year. A cold spasm of pain trickled through his swollen gut.

"And so I'm to stay here." Her nostrils flared. "I'm to clean and cook and sweep like a coolie. To care for your children, to starve and worry, while you – what?"

"While I work," he said. He had an urge to hit her back, to damage her; for a moment he knew how Harun had felt. "I have a long list today. Heart bypasses," he added. Why should she care?

She wrenched past him and pulled at the door. "You..." Her lips worked as words rushed past too quickly for her to say. She plucked the best like shiny, flapping fish, and threw them into the air.

"Everything bypasses *your* heart!"

Left alone in the sudden silence, he stared out of the grimy window. In the distance he could see the KL skyline, glittering through a brownish haze. The city had shone just like that five years ago too, when he'd first arrived in Malaysia with Priya and the two children. *Three* children, he corrected himself. Not two. Not two. Little Bala – dead six months beforehand in a tumbled, half-silent Delhi road collision – had moved with them. He'd moved in the folds of Priya's white saris, in the stillness of the other two children, in Arjun's own swelling flesh and its glacial aches.

"Bala," he whispered. "You're not welcome any more. Go away, little god, please."

"Daddy?" His daughter Asha peered around the door, her round face fretful. Rajan padded behind her, smaller and weaker. Arjun watched as Asha stood on tiptoe to pull a box of cereal down from the cupboard. She didn't look at him as she poured it into two bowls, giving one to her brother.

"I'll take you to school today," he said, willing an answering smile or a giggle or even a few childish tears. "Amma isn't well."

Asha nodded. "And who will pick us up then? Amma? Or you?" Asha's safe passage home – whether by mother or father – had to be decided before she would leave the house. If she remembered Bala at all, Arjun thought, it was only as a dire warning. Asha needed to know how she'd get back, in case – like baby Bala – one day she might not.

"It'll be me," he said firmly. "I'll pick you up."

Priya would be locked in her room all day, sweating, unbathed and rank with misery. By the time he came home she would be calmer, exhausted enough to let him in. He'd lie next to her, he knew, saying nothing but pinching her thin flesh until it blotched and reddened. He gave her small sorrows, at those times, to drown the bigger ones.

"Get your bags and come to the car," he snapped at the children. They flinched and he wished he'd taken them in his arms instead, spent two minutes longer over breakfast. He'd always pushed them too far, or not far enough. He'd always got them wrong.

Outside, he could feel the dirty weight of air settling around him. Asha and Rajan were silent while he drove to the school, and as soon as he stopped the car Rajan disappeared into a giggling, pushing scrabble of infants. Asha stood apart, watching her father leave as though she needed to be sure Arjun had gone before she moved.

At the hospital there were several cases on his list. A heart bypass – he thought unwillingly of Priya – a coronary stent to be put in, a clogged artery to be teased free. And then, just before lunch, an emergency: a child lying still and smooth and blue as Krishna on the table. The surgeon pressed down on the boy's ribs, massaged that helpless heart, and after a few seconds the child began to breathe again. The boy turned pink and plump and healthy, and as everyone in theatre smiled, Arjun looked away. It was hard, he thought, to see Krishna go.

"It's so humid! And the air conditioning just makes it worse." Ben was English, his vowels flat, as though someone had his throat in a stranglehold. He and Arjun were sitting at a scratched plastic table in the cafeteria. Lightweight moulded chairs creaked beneath their weight and the floor was scrubbed clean of shadows.

"It'll get worse." Arjun pulled at his collar. The hospital scrubs were tight under his arms and clung to the inside of his thighs. He gripped his temples, a headache swimming silently below his thoughts, and glanced towards the cafeteria window.

In the far distance he could see a bright-orange figure, hopping and kicking its way over a tattered roof. It looked festive from here, like a spinning top or wind-up toy.

"What's that?" he said, pointing out of the window.

Ben frowned, pinching his lower lip. "I don't know. There's only a car park and the prison there. Do you think it's a patient?"

The figure jigged across a roof and dropped to the ground. A few seconds later it reappeared, climbing the steps of the fire escape to the next building.

"It's getting closer." Ben gnawed at his fingernail. The cafeteria began to fall silent as heads turned towards the window.

A head popped up from the low roof beneath the cafeteria, grinning in through the glass. Arjun saw a buzz cut, a hand grasping at the iron fastenings, a vicious slap at the window that reminded him of Priya.

"He's trying to get in!"

A siren blared suddenly, a muddled raw noise that rushed over them. "Internal evacuation," said the automated voice, calm as a temple pool. "Internal evacuation."

There was a pause, a second of breathless calm before people began to panic. An elderly patient, taken to the cafeteria for a treat by his relatives, whimpered in betrayal and clutched at his untouched food. Nurses fled with quiet efficiency and the smiles slid from the faces of the catering staff.

A security guard pushed into the room against the crowd. "Out!" He was plump-faced, with mild eyes. Arjun had seen him before, greeting cars with a smile as he sat and ate sweets in his guard station. But now his eyes rolled in his head and fear damped his shirt.

"What is it?"

"We don't know. Someone from the prison, perhaps." The guard edged to the door, beckoning him with frantic, flexing fingers. "Sir, please come. You need to evacuate. Go!"

They gathered in the hospital basement, down five flights of stained concrete. Questions sputtered up the stairwell, flooding Arjun's ears.

"Is he in the hospital?"

"He was on the roof, a guard saw him coming."

"Did you see, at the cafeteria window –?"

"The police are here now. They'll catch him."

"But when can we go?"

The guard shook his head. "We've been told to stay here. This man is on the roof, and" – he shrugged – "we cannot leave."

An hour had passed, a dim stretch of boredom and discomfort lit by bright crackles of noise from the guard's radio. A woman soothed her baby, and two men were playing cards.

Ben had been scratching nervously at his mouth, and the dry skin peeled from his lips. "Hope they find him soon," he joked. "Or we'll be down here forever."

Arjun thought about that, carefully. *Forever.* The clean tiled floor would be smeared with blood and urine. The two men playing cards would have fought over the last bottle of water, snatched from a Chinese thoracic surgeon pleading through smashed teeth. The baby would claw at its mother and she'd slap it – give it a black eye – he thought with a strange, aching memory. *But I used to be a god.*

"I'm going out," he said.

Ben looked at him in surprise and Arjun repeated it, louder. He was standing now, moving towards the door with deliberate steps.

"What? Arjun, it was a joke! Calm down, tiger." Ben was half laughing, but Arjun could hear the fright beneath. You're just like me, he thought. You're all just like me, more's the shame.

The security guard moved in front of the door as he reached it. "Sir, please return. You're not allowed to –"

"I have children!" Arjun clutched at this. He had children; he was still a father. "I have to pick them up from school. Let me out!"

The guard shook his head in bewilderment and Arjun, spurred on by fear and a spreading excitement – if only Priya, Bala, Harun could see him now – balled his fist up and punched the man weakly in the centre of his chest. A sharp exclamation came from behind him.

"Hey!"

He flailed for the door handle as Ben grabbed at him, and he kicked backwards. Red hair, he thought, poor Ben. Black hair and a schoolbag in a gutter and a tiny boy under the wheels of a car: poor Arjun. There was a yelp as his foot hit someone, and a recoil, giving him just enough time to pull the door open. In a second he had slipped through and slammed it shut behind him. Blurred shouts came from inside the room, but nobody tried to follow him.

"What the hell? What just happened?"

"Let him go!"

"Arjun! What's going on? Wait…"

He scurried away, head down and counting the corridors as he passed. *Leave a trail*, he thought. *If you don't know how to get back, then perhaps one day you won't.*

At the end of the stairs he began to climb, wiping sweat off his face and adjusting his too-tight scrubs. He remembered his face, years ago, in that mirror in his father's home. Glass-green bones, he'd seen, and a god looking back at him.

All the doors had been left open on the main floor, dark as gaps in teeth. He stumbled along a recovery wall and caught sight of a mirror set into a bathroom nook. His face was pale, doughy and small. No trace of bones, not even under the skin. He was whispering to himself in snatched gulps: prayers he remembered from the oil-lamp darkness of his father's study in Delhi, a nursery rhyme Rajan learnt at school, a list of thoracic disorders from his failed examination.

Turning the corner, he saw light coming from a window in an iron door. A dusty terraced roof was visible through the reinforced glass. As he approached the door he saw a figure in scrubs, translucent and wavering somewhere within the glass. It moved to meet him as he stepped forward, with its lips pulled back in an uncertain smile. It had a doughy, pale face that was transparent, showing the glass-green bones beneath.

He stretched out a trembling hand to the door. He'd thought it would be locked, slammed shut as part of the evacuation, but it opened easily. He stepped out into the thick evening air. In the distance, KL winked in the fading light, skyscrapers coming alive with a pinkish sunset gleam. The man was nowhere to be seen.

Arjun twisted his fingers together, feeling sweat bloom between his legs. When he turned around he saw the door click shut. It locked from the inside and somewhere in the dim corridor he saw the same transparent figure. A god, a green and sharp god, and when Arjun took a step back the god retreated too.

"Nobody knows I'm here." Arjun grinned back at the figure, whose white teeth shone with an incongruous joy. Of course they didn't. If Priya's papery kiss that morning had been a little deeper – if five years ago Bala had followed a safe trail back home – then those shards of glass would still be buried under slumped and greying flesh. Nobody would know.

Arjun peered over the side of the terrace, holding tightly onto the concrete. Three floors down he could see a crowd of people being ushered out by policemen. The sound of reassuring voices drifted up to him.

"They found him, then," Arjun whispered, but nobody replied.

The figure was still watching him, with its face now creased in disappointment. At his feet a puddle of rainwater gleamed a dull pewter in the dying light and he wished the god could see it, too. But all he was doing was watching Arjun, watching him back away to the edge of the terrace. Watching him put one foot over, balancing it on the empty, luminous air. Watching him breathe, swinging the other leg over and sitting poised above the crowds.

In a few minutes, Arjun knew, one of them would leave. Perhaps it would be the god, fading away into the gloom of a corridor to leave nothing but police enquiries, tomorrow's list, Priya and the two children and the tomorrow after that. Or perhaps the god would stay, would watch Arjun's sudden, plunging leap. A leap where Bala would leave him for the first time in years. Where Priya would turn to him with bloodied lips and a final smile, where his three children would look up with hope from their lonely seat outside the school. Where he might, with luck and a following wind, find a trail for his safe passage home.

For You Are Julia

By noon, I'm polishing the phone. The front room's been tidied and all the little smears of living carefully swept away. My rubber gloves are dancing above the sunlit emerald carpet, and God's in his heaven and all's right with the world. And then the phone rings with a little shrill of complaint, as if to say that unlike everything else in here it needs something more than hot yellow sunshine and Pledge.

"Julia?" It's a voice I don't recognise. "It's Tom here."

He pauses. I remember his silence, even though I'd forgotten his voice. I stand in my polished-clean room, feeling quiet spill from the phone and looking at a stain on the carpet. It's a big splotch, right under the sideboard, and I've never noticed it before.

"It's me," I say. "I mean, it's Julia."

I can hear him smile. "Then I've found you at last! I'm having some homecoming drinks tomorrow in the Orchard. Why don't you come? Edward too, of course."

This is a bad idea; a stained-carpet, dust-and-dirt idea. The worst idea, in fact, since Tom once asked me to marry him. Or perhaps only the worst since I refused.

"I'm afraid we can't." I'm brisk, I'm combed and buttoned in my housecleaning slacks and rubber gloves. "Edward always plays tennis on Saturdays."

"Just you, then. Please, Julia," and his voice cracks. They're dangerous, those cracks; I might slide into them and tumble forever. A fallen woman; it's dangerous at my age.

After a few moments I agree, and as I put the phone down, the room darkens. Perhaps it's only a cloud, or perhaps the room itself disapproves. I'm too old for playing games, the tin of Pledge tells me, and the dust-rag adds that I'm certainly old enough to know better. It's only a favour, I insist, and the room pulls itself together a little, clicks its heels. We keep up the standards, this room and I.

I put the phone down and watch Edward outside the window, deadheading roses with mathematical snips. If I look the other way I can see myself in the mirror, pushed rod-straight into my court shoes and the top of my hair bobbing against the frame. This is all as it should be, and I am slotted into my place like a hip bone into a socket – and so it can only be Tom's fault that I want to pull off those silly pink gloves and caper past the windows on nylon feet.

It's dark by the time Edward comes in, a soft and heavy summer dark with crickets stuttering in the dry grass. There's a full moon too, rising treacle-slow past the bedroom window. Old gold light spills over the jagged eaves, but Edward draws the curtains before it can get into the house.

After dinner I tell him about the phone call, quiet as the ice that shifts in his whisky glass. It's civilised, that ice. Just like the pair of us.

"Won't you be bored, dear?" he asks. "It must be years since we've seen the man."

"His retirement do at the hospital, remember? Before he went off to – Sudan? Somalia?"

"Oh yes, the mercy missions." Edward winks at me as he finishes off the whisky. He's not exactly against charity, but he doesn't go in for it in the same way. Edward is a reasonable man.

We've been married thirty years – one flesh, as the marriage service has it – and a single look at him polishes up my nails and tightens my waistband. If this were Tom next to me, I think, we would not be tidied, this room and I. My thighs would press against each other, my stomach would roll over and gobbets of golden light would stream through the smeared glass windows.

I scrub the plates for longer than usual that evening. My fingers are snug in their rubber skins and the kitchen sparkles with a cosy, sudsy light. I'm glad Edward keeps the thick curtains closed, because out there everything's flying free and I can feel moonlight buttered over the fields.

Edward heads off for tennis early the next morning. He keeps himself up, sharp and clean and coloured-in right to the edges. I clean the house, blurring my own edges with thoughts that won't quite stay away. When everything is shining, when I'm ironed and folded and scrubbed to a glowing pink nub, I go into the bedroom and get changed.

As an afterthought, I buckle on shoes that never quite suited me, narrow red heels that tip off-centre.

Outside, everything's soaked in a damp summer heat. Past the low stone walls I can see the cemetery with its tomb to the unknown soldiers, can see sheep lying shipwrecked in the fields and cyclists streaming along the road to Grantchester. I touch my hair, pull my stomach in, trip in my unsuitable blood-red shoes over the arched stone bridge. In the distance, water meadows flatten and steam.

Tom and I first went to the Orchard forty years ago on an autumn afternoon, with leaves gusting tiger-bright about our feet. I was homesick, I remember. I missed the fens, missed the watery light that seeped across the sky and into blue-green fields. I missed the rocking, splashing bogs and the mud and the way the light lay in stripes among the cabbages. I sat in the Orchard a lot back then, writing poetry and waiting for the water lilies to flower in their murky pools. Not now, though. Nowadays I scrub my nails and count my blessings before they're hatched.

And now, too, Tom is waiting for me under the trees. He sits in a hollow where the apple-blossom's begun to blister into fruit and he sags slightly, like muslin with the starch gone out of it. For a moment I'm disappointed. But then he turns to me and smiles. He's holding a bunch of roses, loose and overblown with their petals drooping. I don't see roses like that too often; Edward deadheads them promptly. Tom's different. He's not the kind for a mercy killing.

Tom rings again the next day and invites me to lunch. He calls too early and so I stumble to the phone, leaking dreams and resolutions and the scorched smell of bad teeth. I had my excuse ready last night – Tom, why don't you play tennis with Edward instead; why don't you bring a girlfriend, or better yet, a wife; why don't you, in fact, simply slink off into my past like the water lilies and the poetry – but this morning it's gone. It's been spat out with my toothpaste, with the shreds of Tom I've chewed all night, with the crust of my morning toast and the jam of Edward's kiss.

"I'd love to come," I say instead.

And I know that this will be my summer; the telephone ringing in the hot, fresh mornings while the front room gathers dust. And every evening I'll go to bed alone with Edward, while cats slink close-bellied and yowling on the moonlit roofs. And somewhere in the greying rinds of the night, I'll find a place that's high and tight, a clear place where everything stills then shatters like ice.

"Nice day, dear?" Edward and I are eating supper, both of us fresh from our baths.

"Oh, this and that." I'm casual, as though I barely care. "Tom's been organising a few more walks, history things really. I thought I'd go along tomorrow."

"Rather you than me, dear, if you don't mind me saying. Still" – and here he stops a moment, then carries on bravely – "it's a good interest, history…"

"… there's a lot of it about," I finish, and he chuckles with relief and spoons some cabbage onto my plate, and for a moment this, like the hot yellow sunshine and the Pledge, is all I need.

It won't last, though. Tomorrow night I'll tell him about our walk. I'll tell him about canals, and I'll tell him about medieval villages and National Trust ironworks. But I won't tell him how forty years ago Tom and I wandered hand in hand through those villages, or how he once proposed under the sooty arch of those smelters. I won't tell him how a storm uprooted the sky, how it rained petals and leaves and great gusts of chilled fenland air as we clung together under a beached canal boat. Those things have nothing – or perhaps everything – to do with my husband.

And then it's a day in late summer, a day reefed with heaped white clouds, and Tom is ringing me again. He invites me for lunch in a pub we used to go to, a place we loved so much we had our first fight there. He seems to have forgotten that part.

When we get there it turns out there's a new beer garden, all concrete and Union Jacks and splotched black cigarette marks. The roses over the door have gone, replaced with cut-price fairy lights and televisions showing Sky Sports. There's a family at the next table, ten or so children with a round of tubby adults and a mean little Jack Russell. One of the children has a cake and there's a great to-ing and fro-ing with candles, sparklers and, eventually Happy Birthday, with everyone coming in round-robin late.

"It's so… different somehow, Tom. Don't you think?"

I'm nervous, thighs tense against the splintered seat and my patterned silk skirt catching on snags. If I were with Edward we'd have left by now, and driven home lassoed close with disapproval. But I'm with Tom, whose cheer keeps me at arm's length. He smiles at me, beats time on the table, and finishes off the verse.

"I don't think so," he says, then adds – as though this is an explanation – "You look lovely sitting there. So happy. You're like another woman."

I don't say anything in return. Perhaps another woman would.

After lunch we go for a walk by the village pond. The water snails freeze as our shadows fall on them, shrink back tight against the mud. They can die that way; shrivel up too long into the ooze until they starve and float to the sunlit surface. Byron used to swim here, Tom tells me, pleased with himself. I don't say anything, and watch the sun on water clogged with weeds and rusting tin cans.

We sit on a stile by the pond and Tom turns to face me.

"I'm leaving at the end of the month," he says abruptly. "I told them I'd go back. To the field, the mobile hospital."

There's a pause and he blinks, screwing his face up against the afternoon light. "I wondered if you'd ever thought of heading out yourself. They could always do with someone to keep records. Organise things."

Tom sees nothing but joy, as the hymn puts it. He squints into the sun and sees another woman, and he never dreams it's only me; only Julia tricked out with sunbeams and cataracts. He can't be trusted, or perhaps I can't, and either way it's hopeless. I tell him I can't; I tell him I won't; I tell him that some things never come true. Byron didn't swim here, in any case, I add, that's just a myth they tell to the tourists, and then Tom turns away and lets my hand go.

A breeze has sprung up by the time we leave the stile, bringing the smell of stubbed-out cigarettes and a sodden roar from the television. The clouds are sinking lower and the sun lopes over the water meadows.

We aren't speaking, and haven't been for a while. Perhaps that's why we take a wrong turn, crossing the lane and coming out early, by the village church. A group of women stand outside, their hips uneasy in dove-grey satin, and two starched young men guard the door. They call out as we approach.

"Are you the bride's side or the groom's?" one asks.

Tom's in the middle of an excuse, an apology for someone else's mistake, when I interrupt.

"Bride's," I reply, and he gives a start of surprise. I'm dizzy, though, and need to sit down. To catch my breath, somewhere Tom and I have never been before. A wedding, it might seem, would be the obvious choice.

Inside the church it smells of the cold, of dust and prayers silted up over the narrow glass panes. I slide into a pew and wait. My hair is combed and my shoes are polished, but somewhere inside me there's another woman, who's done with all that. She's done with polish – done with cabbages and pink rubber gloves – and she's yearning for the mud, for storms and filth and the tiger-striped sunsets of Sudan.

But then the organ begins to wheeze, and the bride comes pacing towards us. She's veiled in lace and trussed up in silk, and her feet are squeezed in blood-red shoes. The church is silent in a bright, bitter pause, and outside the summer day is ending. Suppers will be cooling in rooms scrubbed bare and clean as hearts, and curtains drawn against the fading light. Tonight, cats will howl on moon-slick roofs, apples will blister from trees and dew will frost the fields pale grey. Tom will fly away and I will lie next to Edward in all my tidy flesh, and eat cabbage for winter after winter, until one day I grow so old I never even flinch at news reports from Sudan, or Somalia, or anywhere else at all.

Clay for Bones

"Nothing much changes," Sweta whispers, and after being dead for fifty years she should know. Her ashes were scattered in the Periyar river on a rainy Kerala day, with sea fog fleecing the water and the karimeen fish swishing their tails like butter churns. Perhaps that's why she likes this chilly Welsh sun, why she settles her softening thighs on the bench and sucks her teeth with contentment. Pale spring light filters over the grassy hills to drip onto the hospital, over the school across the road and down Sweta's upturned face.

Sweta is my Ammuma, my sepia-toned grandmother in a gorgeous, gold-threaded sari that she'd never have worn in real life. She died in Ernakulam twenty years before I was born; she has spices in her skin and sea-salt in her blood and she's not really here, of course – not in the same way that the hospital is, or the bench, or the shifting bulge of my belly. She's been not-really-here for three weeks now, ever since we shuffled together out of the IVF clinic into a shabby grey morning that brightened wherever it touched her.

"Listen carefully, child," she'd begun, and linked her arm through mine. The pair of us edged splay-footed and wide-bellied past the terraced pit cottages, both too polite to point out that she should have turned up anywhere but here. Back in Cochin I'd understood the ghosts; I'd smelled uppuma at midnight when long-dead aunts took to frying on a cold stove, and nodded to shadowy uncles grateful to skulk in the dim, mosquito-netted corners of the vast bedrooms. But here in Wales the ghosts are different. Sweta doesn't cook, she smells of camphor and old clothes, and she's brimful of a gulpy, finger-wagging ingratitude.

"These doctors are all the same," she'd said on our way home. "They don't know how to finish what they've started."

They didn't need to. I was finishing it all by myself, according to the doctor. My slackened dark skin and briny blood were inhospitable; my tropical womb was choking its tiny Welsh invader.

For weeks before that my food had been coming straight up again, as though something inside were throwing it back. I'd washed up untouched plates each evening, dipping them in suds and rattling worries together with the knives and spoons. *Clay for a baby's bones,* they used to say back home, *and sand for the skin.* But my cravings were more vicious than that, and I'd choked down great mouthfuls of my own fingernail clippings and mats of hair scraped from my plastic razor. After three days I'd rung the hospital: no, Nurse, not an emergency, well perhaps just a little bleeding sometimes – perhaps the doctor could…? The nurse had booked me in with a cool, watery interest that muscled its way through all my good manners.

The doctor had been cautious, frowning at his mint-bright screen where my womb lay cross-sectioned and pinned in place. Something wriggled in its dark glass centre, a sea slug scarred with useless veins.

"And you've named her already, isn't that right, Miss Nair? Baby... Gouri." His tongue had pushed a little at our names, straining them through his moustache. "I'm afraid there may be a problem."

And that's when Sweta first appeared, fading out of the wallpaper as though she'd been there all along. Her feet were stuck into oversized chappals and she had a blue woollen cardigan bundled over her dupatta. She barely glanced at me as she began to write with her flaking nails on my jellied skin. *Blind*, she wrote, *backwards, deaf and deformed.* The doctor frowned at his screen again, and the smile ran off the sides of his face. *Monster*, Sweta wrote, but it was too late to help any of that and so I put my knickers on again and for days afterwards I chewed at my fingernails and gulped them down, because my monster would need to grow claws.

And now we're here for a second scan, waiting outside the hospital on a chilled morning bright with diffident sunshine. A few pale daffodils nearby are bullet-hard and early, pushing up between the lines of an abandoned railway. The tracks bump blindly under our feet, then wind like an unfurled ribbon between the splashing canal and the young green of the hills. This was a mining town years ago, when

Cochin was a fishing village and Sweta was alive and monsters were drowned at birth. The town's been scrubbed up and glossed-over since then; a hospital and a university have been built and a smile's been pasted on the rest of it. But the mines are still there, though, in a way. They're there in the crazy cracked streets that scramble uphill, in the grassed-over slagheaps and in the ornamental lake where toy boats sail over a sunken pit shaft.

Across the road a school slumps in a desert of asphalt, dotted with portable classrooms and sliced up by iron gates. The grounds are swarming with perfect two-legged, two-eyed children, and soon it will be time for Sweta to lead me through the hospital gates. We will walk past the roundabout with its naked flagpole, past the little glass smoker's huts and the half-built hospice wing, and up the steps to the Imaging Department, where the doctor will frown, then forget my monster-baby's name.

"You cheated, Bron!"

Two girls come bounding out of the open school gate and up to the road. They're throwing a shiny rubber ball to each other and counting out different sets of catches and claps in a game that looks far too young for them. Their voices are shrill, and I wonder if Gouri will ever be able to catch, or clap, or count.

"I didn't! I finished sixsies before you got to school, so I'm on fivesies now."

Their limbs skitter like daddy-long-legs; they have hiked up skirts and smudged glittery nail polish and voices that are just a little bit too loud.

"And these," Sweta says with disapproval tinging the edge of her voice, "do you think *these* will be her friends?"

The girls have started to squabble noisily, a poisonous argument of the sort I remember from my own school days; the sort that lingered on our skirts and salted our dal with spite. They're back-talking, blonde-hair, cigarettes-behind-the-bike-shed girls; and Gouri will need them as friends, if only because they're nothing like me.

"God, you're a retard, Bron." One of the girls snorts a disdainful sip of air. Bron has just missed an easy catch, and the ball plops round and smooth onto the fat of her thighs before rolling underneath my feet.

"Hey, Miss!" Bron flickers a Siamese-cat glare at me and demands, "Pass us the ball back?"

It's rolled into the gutter and I have to scrabble for it among the crisp packets and dried-out dog messes. There's something soft too, a velvet that brushes against my torn fingernails, and I snatch back my hand. Under all that rubbish is a dead bird, a little farmyard chick a week or two old. Its yellow fluff is blackened and gummy and its face has been smashed to shards of bone. A breeze slips across the playground and its stubby wings lift in a wary shiver, as though it might still fly. The girls start to giggle, a smothered and chesty sort of sound, and one of them whispers, "She touched it!"

The ball's next to it, filthy with mud and pimpled with glass from a shattered bottle. The girls catch my eye and shriek softly, their bodies clutching inwards with laughter, and I grit my teeth and kick a fold of newspaper over the entire mess.

"Come up, child, come and walk." Sweta pulls at me with a scolding concern. Bron throws us a fluttering, barbed smile as they cross the road, and Sweta clicks her teeth together.

"Those girls are alley cats, child, all teeth and spit."

She pats the material over my belly straight with a vicious, punishing sort of a smack. I'm wearing a gaudy shalwar kameez today – it's all that will fit – and I feel self-conscious in all that clamour of pink and scarlet. Sweta stumps wordlessly by my side, pulling her cardigan close against the thinness of the wind.

As I cross the road I can see a tangle of streets knotted around grim little gathering-points. A parade of little shops, a concrete playground, a dark brown and silent community hall. At the end of the terrace a faded newsagent sign lies propped above a litter of handwritten notices: homeless dogs, lost handbags and missing children all forlorn behind the soaped-over windows. Next to it a gleaming green-and-white supermarket looks out of place, overdressed for the occasion. On the other side there's a dusty one-room shop. It seems to sell everything – pet food, hardware, second-hand clothes and thick slabbed hamburgers in polystyrene boxes. A trickle of customers spill out onto the road, hurrying off as though ashamed of having been there in the first place.

There's a tired smell coming out from its door, a smell of twice-cooked grease that turns my stomach milky and cold. In the window I see the hospital, crouched below the grassy slagheaps like a dirty brick spider. Something jerks behind the glass, and I look up quickly.

Inside the window there's a cage full of young chicks, twitching in the steaming air. They're placed on a shelf behind a glass plate, and next to them a glittery hand-lettered sign reads "Cheep! to good homes". The glass is covered with congealed handprints and slicked with a thin film of breath and grease from the customers waiting in an impeccable, dreary line.

"Do you remember the cockfights?" Sweta asks, and starts to scrape with her yellowing fingernail on the window. *Monster*, she writes, and the largest chick starts to flap. It fastens its beak onto the neck of a smaller one and hunkers it down within range of the tiny dewclaws.

The cockfights were held in the afternoon markets in Cochin when I was a child, next to our school. We heard them start each week, a roar that grew while we sat under the creaking, ticking fans in our clean white blouses. I remember loose-lipped Tamils swaggering up the road with scraggy hook-clawed birds tied under their arms, and our teacher sweeping the shutters closed with a clash of bangles on her plump wrists. We sat in the sun-striped gloom all afternoon, and by the time we went home there was only a circle of dust soaked with spilt toddy and a strange, musky stain.

"When I was young, they used to set stray cats to fight the cocks," Sweta says. "I trapped the back alleys and sold the cats, one rupee each. They were scrawny things, half-blind with mites, and I never believed they would lose."

The chicks in the shop are quiet now, cowering down on the newspaper that lines their cage. A hand reaches in, fumbling at the soft yellow fluff, and drags one out by its neck. The chick rakes a thin seam of blood across those fingers, then it's banged smartly against the cage door and pulled up out of view.

A second later a schoolgirl shoulders out of the shop, trailing a mix of sweat and deodorant like the tail of a comet. It's Bron, with her slit-blue eyes, her pitted skin and her hair in a living clump at the base of her neck. She's squeezing her fingers tight around the flapping, choking chick.

She stares at me as she passes, a sliding glance that bumps off my belly and skates over my swollen pink-draped ankles. At the edge of the road she squats down and drops the chick onto the ground with a brisk brush of her hands. It kicks and claws at her thick, doubled-up thighs and her slouching ankle socks before she pushes it forward into the road and stands up. She walks back towards the shop, the chilly light falling slantwise on her cheekbones, on her springing hair and on the finger she sucks methodically.

"I've let it go!"

But she doesn't look interested, not really, as though what happens next could hardly have anything to do with her.

A wind swirls at the roots of my hair, and over the rim of the hill I see a bus beginning to pick up speed. A tongue of chilled air snakes out in front of it and wraps around the chick, huddled tight against the asphalt.

My monster kicks and then I'm up, my feet smacking on the pavement as I run to snatch the chick away. The bus looms above us both in a shaking roar of metal, and I feel Sweta's hand slide into my own. Her fingers brush along the lines of my palm, along the loveline and heartline I've carried all the way from Cochin, and she digs her flaking nails into my skin. She tugs at me, leaving a jagged scratch that scores through all those lines, and then there's a raw slap of cold and the bus is gone.

The wind dies down and in the gutter the layers of rubbish sigh and settle. Bron straddles the kerb, her eyes slit crocodile-thin and a smirk hidden beneath her lips. Behind her I see Sweta's writing gleam on the window: *Monster*.

"She will need to be," Sweta says, and touches my belly. I take a step towards her and then another and then I'm shuffling away from Bron and her smile and the soaped-over, missing children. I go back to the bench where I was sitting, and kneel with Sweta in the thin mud. Together we sift through the rubbish until I find Bron's missing ball, a grimy sphere of rubber sticky with filth. One day, I think,

Gouri will cheat at sixsies. I wipe the ball clean and tuck it into my shalwar kameez pocket. The fragments of glass zip and rub against the nylon, quiet as uppuma frying on a midnight stove.

"Hey!" Bron shouts from across the road, and her voice sounds tinny, its edges scraped off. "You can't just fucking take…"

I turn my face up to the sky, where the light drips and fleeces like the sea fog in Cochin. The clouds have burnt off now, and there's a brittle smell in the air: a smell of spring turning over in the valleys. The wind bites into my ears, licking me with frost and the palest sunlight. It's as cold as sand, as cold as empty mines and the clay beneath the Periyar river. I bite off a shred of fingernail, swallow it with love, and turn towards the hospital gate.

The Names of Things

"So he decided the art wasn't *realistic* enough." Robert champed on that, as though somewhere inside it might have a harmless core. "Sydneysider, he was. Shoes polished clean as his arse, and ten to one he'd never even met a bloody Abo."

Robert had met me at the airport, nodding from behind the luggage carousel. He was a nugget of a man, with nicotine-stained hair and a leathered face dry as dubbin wax. When he'd settled into the driving seat of his car he'd spread his legs with satisfaction and a kind of grinding contentment.

"So I told him where to get off." He rammed the ute up a gear to guide us over a rise, and in the valley ahead I saw silvery mirages flicker and run. "Sold them *elsewhere*."

But he looked away, and something in the way he said *elsewhere* made me think he was lying. Robert was a postcard artist, turning out delicate sketches of bunchy-cheeked Aboriginal children flawless as dollies. They were charming, those dollies, with their bush tucker walks and their games of footy. I'd seen some of the cards at the airport, glossy white strips in a "Welcome to Western Australia" travel pack.

"You here for work, then, love?" His eyes were slitted as they caught the gleam of streetlights. We'd driven through outer suburbs barnacled with hardware stores and retail parks, and were heading east now into a wash of indigo sky. Lantanas crept close, holding up clusters of vivid, heatless flowers, and in the distance blackboys shook like monstrous porcupines.

I nodded. "Anthropology fieldwork." I saw him frown. "Studying family relationships, Aboriginal customs. That sort of thing."

I'd found his name tacked up on the university noticeboard when I was looking for a local hotel. Robert and Marie Gundarsson, with an address and an offer of airport transport thrown in. Someone had added a spidery note: *Good host, once you get used to him.* And that was that, leaving me to walk around the sentence and wonder just what it was I'd be getting used to.

"Families, hah! Bloody weird, if you ask me. They won't even say someone's name after he dies, those Abos."

He smacked the word fruitily off his tongue and I coughed, my knees knocking together in their stiff new jeans. Next to Robert I felt prissy, felt soaped and civilised, as though my teeth were too large and white in my mouth.

"It's just... research, mate," I said in the end, flabby as a boiled egg.

"Research." He leant back, steering with the tips of his fingers. "Waste of time, Net. There's no original thought now; no original thought."

He called me Net instead of Annetta, as though I were a trap spread out to catch him, and glanced over with a sneaking, no-flies-on-me smirk. The blackened twists of spinifex jostled behind our wheels, and somehow I drifted off to sleep and then woke again to hear Robert sigh, "No original thought."

By the time we pulled up at his house it was dark, and our shadows were faint tidemarks under the yellowing streetlights. Robert limped up the cracked path. I'd noticed at the airport that one leg was shorter, but the way he moved made the deformity seem new, as though his limb had shrivelled during the drive. From inside I could hear a hiss of steam and a muffled, sudsy clatter.

"Marie!"

A woman came out onto the boarded verandah steps, bleached grey against the kitchen light. She sniffed and wiped her nose before offering me a hesitant hand.

"Sorry, love. It's these onions." She gestured back helplessly into the kitchen as Robert climbed the stairs, landing a jolly, smacking kiss on her slipping smile.

"Maybe I should have washed them first or something…" Her voice trembled with weariness, with an exhaustion that pulled at her slackened skin. There was a smell of cheap perfume and under that, a sort of soaped-clean sickness.

"We've put you in the sleep-out, Annetta." She clawed at her scalp with her fingertips, wincing a little. "Get freshened up and I'll see about tea."

The sleep-out was at the back of the house, separated from the verandah by a folding partition. Someone had tried to turn it into a guest room, with apricot-crocheted clothes hangers standing to attention in the plywood wardrobe, but the wool was already thick with dust. One of Robert's pictures lay crumpled on the desk, a half-drawn sketch of white teeth and crinkled black eyes, as though he'd given up before finishing the smile. A fluorescent tube cast sharp blue shadows over everything, filling the room with the knock and sizzle of dying moths. When I switched it off I could see myself in the filmy shadows of a mirror, trembling with a jellyfish frailty.

The kitchen seemed bright after that, a scrubbed and salted place where Marie's onions rolled in the sink like lifebuoys. I heard voices in the living room and found Marie damp-faced and red-eyed, crumpled into a brown velvet sofa. Robert sat stiffly in a matching chair by her side. A tasselled shade swung overhead, casting bobbing shadows over everything except Robert and Marie adrift on their little raft of light.

"Net, right, let's get cracking." Robert jumped up when I came in, bouncing from good foot to bad with his fists raised in an up-and-at-'em salute. "Come up the butcher's and we'll get some snags for tea, eh?"

There was something false about his smile and the way his face strained at it. That smile and the too-loud voice and the chopping fists all seemed flimsy somehow, like the mirages on the road.

"Robert." Marie lay tipped against the sofa arm, with one hand pressed deep into her side. "We've got snags here, no call to go up Joe's." Her voice shook, and she scratched at the driftwood bones of her wrist. "In the deep-freeze, can have them done in two shakes – "

But he was already striding out, leaving her stranded there with her hands clutched in on herself and her eyes raw and swollen. She wiped her cheeks and said in a dry, dirty voice that didn't quite suit her, "You'd better go with him, Annetta. I'll see to those onions."

Robert was waiting outside, by an old wooden shoe rack clotted with spider webs. He picked up one of the boots and shoved his hand deep inside it.

"Know about spiders, Net? Snakes?" he asked, and thrust his face at me with a bullying sort of jeer. "They can't bite in the dark. It's scientifically impossible."

"But…"

"Bullshit, you hear? Scientifically impossible. Those Abos around here, they pick 'em up at night – funnel-webs, tiger snakes, dugites."

But funnel-webs lived only in the eastern states, and Robert's face was twitching as his fingers worked deeper in the shoe.

"Go on, Net." He pushed another boot at me, jerking his head so his throat swelled and dropped like a rooster's crop. "Don't have the guts?"

I took a deep breath and pushed my hand inside the shoe. Something moved, a scrabbling just beyond my fingers, and my heart kicked as a gecko dropped out on the floor.

"Copped it! Should have seen your face, love!"

I put the boot down with shaking hands. Robert's tobacco-slabbed grin was splitting his face, and beneath the kitchen's clatter and steam I could hear Marie sob.

"Robert!"

Spangles of light shone through the blackness outside; a soft yellow porch, a kitchen drained and scrubbed, a blue-white and beseeching bedroom. Bats wheeled across the cross-stitched stars and on the nature strips kangaroos were frozen in the moonlight.

"Look – Marie, she's not feeling so good, right? Shouldn't we stay with her?"

"Nah, she'll be right." He'd brought along a walking stick, thick as a choko vine, and he stabbed it into the crackling grass. "Get a shift on, Net. No point standing round like a coupla pork chops."

We'd come to a short driveway that led past a square brick building and back into the bush. A wind had picked up, twisting the dangling strips of silverbark that gleamed wan among the trees. Behind the building I could see a fenced-in yard that looked like a poultry run, littered with tufted paws of kidney weed. A sandwich board leant against the wall. *Joe's Egg and Meat Shack*.

"Shack, hah. Got that right." He bit the last word savagely, the way he'd said "No original thought."

"Right, Net. Snags, eh?"

The door was splintered, gouged at waist height by a series of jagged pits like the grassy scars from Robert's stick. Fresh paint flaked off around our feet and a latch held the door closed from inside. Robert coughed, then spat cleanly onto the doorstop and reached through the buckled gap to snap the latch free. It looked practised, that twist, and when the door swung open he thrust his shoulders back and shook the stoop out of them like a performer waiting for applause.

Inside was a single, square room, lit by another buzzing fluorescent tube. The walls were glossed white, and the ancient yellow counter had been wiped till it shone. An esky sat near the front, the lid snapped tight on a piece of card. NO TRESPASSING, it read. POLICE NOTIFIED, with each letter level and scalpel-sharp. There was a rustle in the air, a slithery, unsettled sense of movement.

"Bloody Abo shopkeeper." Robert hefted his walking stick and jabbed at the esky, sending it tumbling it to the floor. The lid cracked open, bouncing under the counter to spill out a puddle of greyish water. An enormous huntsman spider skittered out from under the lid and Robert swore, then flipped it on its back into the shallow pool.

"Robert?" The air stirred again, and my voice scraped in my throat. He was standing in the corner by another door, this one hung with dangling strands of plastic to keep out the flies.

"Go on, Net. Out the back, eh?" He sounded gentle now, as though he were asking a favour. His mouth was a chew of raw skin, and though he shuffled his feet loudly, he didn't move away from the door.

Through the plastic strips was a tiny back room, crisp with the dry smell of straw. A throbbing murmur came from a low poultry house along one wall, and opposite it a misted ice-box held scraps of meat and jigsawed bones. The only light came from the main shop, and my shadow threw a blackened length against the far wall. I could feel Robert behind me, his breath sucking damp through his teeth.

"So, Net. Got a boyfriend, back east? Or kids, you got kids?" He shuffled closer, bringing a reek of sweated leather. I took a step away, a tippy-tapped no-offence-meant shuffle that ended up as a panicked scurry. *Once you get used to him*, I thought.

"No, mate." Now I was next to the wall my shadow had shrunk back down to normal size, and the tawny sound of the hens rose and sank with my heartbeat. I folded my arms, faced him square. "How about you and Marie?"

He seemed to sag in on himself, all the swagger crumpling and his hands hanging limp as waterlogged gloves.

"Marie, eh?"

He hobbled over to the corner where the poultry house lay in shadow. "She's crook, Net. Real bad. Something up with her insides, they said. She can't have kids." I could only see his eyes, pale and dimly wet as he sank down against the mesh. He breathed in and held it, like a child left scared in the dark.

"I'm sorry." I hadn't expected to be sorry for him, but something about the way he spoke had sounded scoured and comfortless. "Look, and we've left her all alone, right? Come on, let's get home."

"We had a dog, though." Robert didn't move. "Close enough, eh, Net? Good enough for us." His smile was stretched, with a terrible sort of cheerfulness. In the cage next to him a tumble of warm, brooding feathers stirred and pressed against the wire.

"He was a little scrapper, that pup. Used to come up here to beg for bones, but Joe wouldn't have a bar of it. Said he put the hens off laying. Chased him off with a stick." Robert cracked his own walking stick against the cages, and the birds hissed and fluttered inside.

"And then one day the little fella never come back," he said. "So Marie got on at me after tea to come and have a look here, 'case a snake had got him." He swung his head from side to side with a sort of bullish disbelief.

"Scientifically impossible," I said. It wasn't a joke, not quite, and he nodded at me through the dark with sober gratitude.

"Place was lit up like a cricket pitch when I got here," he said, "Joe's motion lights were on and the chooks were still out. And there was this noise, Net, by the fencepost out back. Like a kid crying." He turned back to the cages with a grimace that showed his brownish teeth.

"There he was, biggest bloody rooster I've ever seen. Big as a fighting cock. And the dog too, trying to dig out a hole to get away. They must've been scrapping, 'cause there was blood thick as guts on the ground. And then the rooster snaps his beak, comes away with a bit of fur and the dog gives this howl. Like he can't do anything but scream."

Robert stopped for a second and slipped his fingers in through the wire mesh. He stroked at the bird's wing almost gently; then with a stiff tug some feathers slipped free. The hen scuffled, hunkered down against the cage floor and I saw his knuckles swell with a jagged scratch.

"By the time I got him out it was too late. Poor little tacker kicked the bucket before we got home."

He looked down at me with the lost look of someone who'd got in amongst the roots of everything, and found it all wanting.

"Marie never mentioned him again, Net. Never even asked how he died."

The fluorescent light through the doorway buzzed and dimmed, and a great soft moth began to splash against the plastic strands. I slipped my arm through the crook of his elbow and felt the tender slick of our skins together.

"Joe bought some postcards off me the next day," he said eventually. "They don't understand, you see. The Abos. They don't have the words for it."

One of the birds in the poultry run squawked, sharp as nails, and I thought of Marie's sliding tears, and of Joe coming back through the silent bush with a clutch of Robert's black-faced dollies. Almost everything Robert had said today had been wrong, had been cross-grained and vicious, and yet there was a sort of salty truth in the feel of his arm through mine.

"Go home, Net," he muttered. Something in the telling had disappointed him, as though he'd expected more of it. He humped himself free, his bad leg stuck out stiff and shrivelled as a cuttlefish bone. Somewhere behind that dry face and chewed-up mouth there were feral, wordless things happening, and as I left his fingers clutched silently at something just out of reach.

Back in the main shop the spider was huddled in a sodden knot against the counter. The door swung loose, letting in a streak of rustling night and the glimmer of a distant streetlight. The nature strips outside were empty now, but above it all the bats still danced and the fog rose grey and bloodless, and the tar-black sky still offered up a slice of moon as though nothing had been its fault.

A few months later someone took Robert's scribbled card down from the university noticeboard. No longer letting rooms, our secretary said as she picked at her teeth, not since his wife died. *Marie*, I said, *her name's Marie*, and the secretary shrugged inside her cardigan as she clipped away down the corridor. They say it brings bad luck, to name the dead, but like Robert I had expected more.

I tried to tell the story to my husband once, when I was first married and beached safe on the sands of my own life. But the freshness had gone from it, and all that was left was the memory of some apricot-crochet hangers in a silent room, and a sense that somewhere we had all gone wrong.

Dust and Spices

"Tell me about when you were a boy, Daddy. In the olden days." Kumar's generous with his questions, in a way that will only last a few more years. He'll soon be too old to call thirty years ago "the olden days", and far too grown-up to ask.

He's been sitting in the kitchen all evening, crayoning luminous yellow suns and trees green as boiled limes. The streets outside are furred with a stealthy English frost and lit by a sodium glare, but Kumar dismisses all that with a regal magnificence as his suns shine on. He would make, I expect, a wonderful emperor.

An hour ago I sent him off to play while I lit the *puja* lamps. I've filled the blue bowl with offerings – sweets and marigolds and oranges bright as a winter sunset – but for once he hasn't tried to rifle it before Lord Shiva gets his chance. That thought prises me away from the stove, and I find him ensconced at my desk, kicking socked feet and steadily ransacking a litter of photograph albums.

"It's me!"

He jabs at a picture of a boy squinting at the camera. It's been taken in front of a low-slung pink house, sprawling like a pavilion with shreds of garden clinging to its sides. The boy looks older than Kumar, and in any case, there's no resemblance, not a particle.

"And these are me, too!"

I look down at the spread of pictures and see he's appropriated every small boy in the album, from his own great-uncle to a child acrobat in an Ipoh circus. Kumar, little god, will not accept rivals.

He follows me downstairs, chattering like a monkey and trying to jam the picture of the boy and the pavilion into my hand. When I take it, I see that there's a woman in it too. She's kneeling behind the boy, with a swirl of bright hair blown over her eyes and a finger to her lips.

"Who's the lady, Daddy…?" The question dies away as he spots the bowl of sweets, and his eyes bulge with longing.

That longing must run in the blood, I think, like theft and love and lies. And since none of that can be helped, I reach over to steal us both a sweet from the gods and tell him, "She's Queen Guinevere."

When I was a boy in Kuala Lumpur, my father would practise yoga on the roof before he left for work. I would watch him from the corner by the dovecotes, my mouth brimming over with questions and my fingers hooked into the twisted wire netting. I remember his stretches, black arcs against the green-gold sky. I remember the smell of breakfast cooking downstairs, remember the heat blown up from the valleys in wisps like feathers, and the traffic starting to roll and ebb in the lanes below. One morning he missed his yoga and I cried behind the kitchen among the touch-me-nots and bleaching fish-pails, because I thought the sun would forget to rise.

"Show the photograph with me, Daddy," I'd say. "With me and the lady."

Every year the summer rains meant power cuts; meant stifling, candle-dark nights when my father forbade reading on pain of blindness. With the blackened bedrooms looming above me and nightmares teeming on the stairs, the family photograph albums were the only way to keep him safely in arms' reach. The picture I wanted was on the front page: a bright-haired lady forever kneeling behind a small boy. The boy wasn't me, not truly – he had my father's hooked nose and wide, wide smile – but that didn't change my mind one bit. He was me in all senses but the least important, and I demanded the photograph with a proprietorial swagger.

That lady's Alice in Wonderland, he'd tell me; she's Alice who fell down the rabbit hole. She tumbled down from the sky and landed right next to you for the photograph! And then she asked you to come and meet the Cheshire Cat – and we'd be off with Alice for hours, until the lights flickered back on and the goblins fled from my bedroom. Every night she was new; she was Alice or Maid Marian, she was Sleeping Beauty or Queen Guinevere, gorgeous as the sunrise.

She scampered out into my dreams on those nights, her hair wild and one finger held to her sepia lips. Next morning I'd go to school, leaving her tucked into the house with my mother, and the toy horse stowed in the attic, and the metal breakfast cups that fitted one into another like chickens into eggs. And, as with all those things, I fell in love.

"Lipis, okay? Last stop, lah." The bus driver was Malay, and English rolled clogged and cold off his tongue. At nineteen I must have been only half his age, but I felt sapped and stiff in my crumpled blazer and flannels. He smacked the horn twice, then spat immensely out of the window.

I stumbled out into a tiny rust-red clearing that steamed in the flat evening sun. Market women trudged across it with baskets balanced on their heads and worries nailed to their feet, while schoolboys skimmed back and forth in ragged clumps like swallows. There was a blurred silence over everything, a smudged quiet tangled with the whirr of crickets and rain slipping down from waxy leaves. Lipis still seemed half-finished, with a few shacks straggling up the hillside above a tiny village raw as a landslip. The houses leading away from the main street were raised on thick stilts and shuttered tight against the evening glare. Dogs lurked in the maze of ladders and rubbish under the town, and from a radio somewhere inside, the call to prayer buzzed with static.

We had passed through here every year when I was small, on our way to celebrate Diwali with my auntie in Penang. As we waited at the station my father would hand a few coins out of the train to the tea-stall woman, and I would flatten my face against the glass, watching her mix the ais down the corridor. They say it brings bad luck, to name the dead, but like Robert I had expected more.

I tried to tell the story to my husband once, when I was first married and beached safe on the sands of my own life. But the freshness had gone from it, and all that was left was the memory of some apricot-crochet hangers in a silent room, and a sense that somewhere we had all gone wrong.

One of the birds in the poultry run squawked, sharp as nails, and I thought of Marie's sliding tears, and of Joe coming back through the silent bush with a clutch of Robert's black-faced dollies. Almost everything Robert had said today had been wrong, had been cross-grained and vicious, and yet there was a sort of salty truth in the feel of his arm through mine.

"Go home, Net," he muttered. Something in the telling had disappointed him, as though he'd expected more of it. He humped himself free, his bad leg stuck out stiff and shrivelled as a cuttlefish bone. Somewhere behind that dry face and chewed-up mouth there were feral, wordless things happening, and as I left his fingers clutched silently at something just out of reach.

Back in the main shop the spider was huddled in a sodden knot against the counter. The door swung loose, letting in a streak of rustling night and the glimmer of a distant streetlight. The nature strips outside were empty now, but above it all the bats still danced and the fog rose grey and bloodless, and the tar-black sky still offered up a slice of moon as though nothing had been its fault.

A few months later someone took Robert's scribbled card down from the university noticeboard. No longer letting rooms, our secretary said as she picked at her teeth, not since his wife died. *Marie*, I said, *her name's Marie*, and the secretary shrugged inside her cardigan as she clipped away

"Your grandfather was born here," I tell Kumar, but at fifteen he's too old for both generosity and theft, and he doesn't even look up. The sun slants flat through the carriage and our shadows stretch out along the ground until they're so tall, as tall as our fathers, but nobody gets out and the train begins to pull away.

Foxgloves

Baby Dayle was born two months ago; it's written right there in the crisp record book Nurse Anderson shoved into Tracey's hands as she left the ward. Birth weight and height percentiles and registered-name-if-you-please-*Miss*-Dayle. Tracey hasn't thought of a name yet, though. Nothing seems to suit him.

She loves this baby, a desperate kind of love that soaks right through her. The kind that's anxious, and grubby, and smells of dirty lino and rancid sweat. The kind that's reflected in a window at night, miniskirt and heels and a teenage voice. *Looking for something, babes?*

Every evening she rocks him to sleep on a cheap plastic chair by the kitchen window. She sees her face reflected in the blackness, drained and white under a bare light bulb. He mewls and kicks, but she doesn't move, just sits there with him and watches the dark.

She traces the way out, though, in her head. Go down to the river, past the twisting maze of narrow grey terraces. Hurry past the pebbledash peeling from high, crooked walls and past the streets plunging again and again down the hill. Past the skips, past the cul-de-sacs of rusting cars and broken prams. Don't look back. Don't look back to the soaped-over shop windows, and the railway cutting choked with rubbish, and the boarded-up Carmelite church that nobody's got any use for, not any more. Not here.

Go down to the river. Cross the bridge. Look up.

It takes her breath, Black Mountain, waiting just past the grimy streets where the world soars up to the sky. It's a gigantic surge of rabbit-nibbled earth, thrown up high enough to catch the wind from the valleys. It's clean up on those heights. Clean as things that laugh in the night, clean as riddles on an empty hillside, clean as blood on a stone.

She's sure there's something living there, flickering and racing across the hills at night, hiding in the slag heaps, laughing from the empty mineshafts and shaking the foxgloves at noon. She's never seen it, but she will one day, she knows. Otherwise, what's the point?

"He's called Merlin?" A pause, a huff of breath through the nostrils, and that's just Tracey's whole life right there, isn't it, wrapped up in a single smirk that lasts a heartbeat. "That's clever, dear."

The huffed breath – snorting away, Tracey thinks indignantly, like Puff the Magic Dragon – belongs to Sandra, her social worker. Sandra's face is powdered, set in folds like stale cake mixture and her mascara-slicked eyes are creased. She's smiling, she always smiles when she visits, but there's a curly little sneer hidden somewhere in her face and a lick of alley cat about her.

"Yes, I've just decided." Tracey won't give an inch. "It's out of King Arthur, you know. Merlin's the wizard."

Sandra's eyes narrow, just slightly. She could be smiling, but Tracey knows better. *Chav*, those eyes are saying, and *dirty cow*, and oh yes, she's comparing her own cold wave dye-and-set to Tracey's velvet-scrunchie ponytail that strains her face tight as skimmed milk. There's something nasty that comes into the room with Sandra; something that smells of the mountain and scuttles behind Tracey's kitchen door.

Tracey chews at her sleeve, the fabric still wet and gummy from her slopped mug of tea, and listens to Sandra. I know what it's like, Sandra's saying, I really do. After all, Tracey recites in her head, wasn't she only nineteen herself when she had little Meg? Of course, it helped to have a good head on her shoulders, and she hopes she's not speaking out of turn, but it's high time Tracey pulled it together, *sorted herself out*. And Tracey nods and clutches the stack of adult education brochures pushed into her hands, and thinks that maybe one day everyone will stop talking at her and over her and it'll be okay just to sit and be Tracey again.

Sandra pushes her chair back, swivels her heavy thighs around with a sound like wet rubber smacking on concrete, and Tracey can't stand it any more.

"What about Robbie?" She sniffs, wipes her nose on her sopping sleeve and stares right at Sandra. "Have you heard anything yet?"

Sandra sighs, letting Tracey know just how patient she's being. "Nothing, love. He's still with the fosters in Swansea, you know that. You've been getting the letters?"

Tracey's heard all this before, refuses to believe anything written in those childish letters, which come postmarked Swansea and signed Robbie but somehow still smell of Sandra's perfume. Sometimes she thinks it's all just a fairy tale wrapped up in an ugly skin; it's King Arthur, or Harry Potter, or the *NeverEnding Story* that used to play on the late-night screenings when she went out on the lash down Merthyr. Her Robbie's been stolen away, but if she fights a dragon and tricks the witches and says just the right words then she'll get him back.

But not today. Today there aren't any magic words, or dragons, or anything except a lifetime of trudging up her terraced street with a pram and a hangover and her mistakes dragging behind like a sodden length of rope. Today there's only Sandra, and Tracey's in tears now, red-nosed and red-eyed and acne flaring out under the chip-shop grease of her skin.

"It's not letters he needs, it's his mother!"

"Hush, hush." Sandra smothers her in a hug, massive arms that smell of sweat and talcum and jiggle like raw meat on the bone. "The Family Court say he's better off with the fosters for a while. Till you sort yourself out, love."

Tracey nods, snuffles a little and slouches over to get some formula from the tin. She doesn't believe a word of it, any more than she believes in changelings, in child snatchers and wicked witches and fairies who steal babies to hide in the rocks up on the Mountain. Which is to say that one story is like another to Tracey, and there's no one left to care which one she picks.

She remembers that night three years ago, but only when she can't help herself. A year after Robbie was born, it was, and all that was left was cold hours by herself on a stained mattress while her world shrank tight and dirty around her. Robbie wouldn't stop howling, she remembers, so she stuffed him into his cot with a bottle of blackcurrant and she was off to find someone else, rough trade or passing trade or any trade at all, because it was better than what she had right now.

And down the wine bar or the clubs it was better, it really was, with the lads from the town who went there for a bit of slumming. Jailbait, they called her sometimes, and chav, just like Sandra – when they thought she didn't hear – but it didn't stop them buying her drinks and she'd often thought they liked it better that way.

But maybe she mentioned Robbie too often, or maybe one of the boys thought better of it afterwards, because there was a call to the child services and then there was Sandra slithering through her door like trouble in a powdered skin.

It was a pity, of course, everyone said. But she hadn't really wanted a kid, though, had she – at her age? And it's not like the da's any use – poor girl doesn't even know who he is – and anyway, it's only till she gets herself back on her feet. That's the story they all told, anyway, and by now Tracey almost believes it herself.

She knows exactly what happened; they like to *keep the birth mother informed*, says the helpful pamphlet that rotted in her kitchen bin. She's heard how two social workers – *highly trained and experienced with family situations* – took Robbie to Swansea, hunching through the rain and over the slippery railway platforms. How the taxi swished them along fuddled, foggy streets to a council centre where a neat young couple waited with Colgate smiles and a Waitrose card and classical music on the stereo, and that's our Robbie landed on his feet, he has.

But Tracey doesn't like that story. She's got another one, even if she can only whisper it to herself in bed when the infomercials are on and she's huddled under the duvet waiting for hours to pass. In this story, those two social workers take Robbie from her; she can't change that. But then they dance straight up the Mountain, up into the streaming mist and the flocks of crows. And they stop up there, high on the grey-green mountain, and rip their skins right off, slicing through the gristle and fat. She knows, in this story, that they were goblins all along; highly trained goblins, of course, experienced with family situations and with good heads on their shoulders.

And in this story Robbie escapes – of course he does – and he creeps deep into the mineshafts hand in hand with the wizards and the orphans and all the other ones who made it out. And, just before she goes to sleep, Tracey tells herself the last part – the part where she says the magic words to bring him back. The part where she follows a trail of foxgloves right out of the valleys and into her own happy ending.

By evening there are frost patterns feathering the window. The house smells of pot, smells of TV dinners and nappies and a bottle that sits curdling in a tepid sanitiser. Tracey lies on the couch with Merlin in her miserable arms, and her gaze slides around the room. Nowhere for her to go except down to the betting shop, but the men there watch her legs as she passes and the girls have tongues that cut her to strips. *Where's she going, then? Down the railway cutting with those boys from Aberfan, no wonder she had the kid took off of her.*

She's nervous, too, always is after Sandra's been. But it's worse now, because something scuttled in with Sandra and it's still here. It's watching her from the chilly cavern out in the hall, whispering to her from the infomercials that flicker over the walls.

She chews at the ragged edge of a fingernail, nibbles at the skin of a ripped cuticle. Her ears are ringing, and a shadow's slipping around the room, just out of sight every time she looks up. There's a can of lager on the table, and she doesn't remember opening it, but she could swear that the last mouthful tasted of flowers.

Through the doorway to the dim hall outside there's a square of greasy mirror lit by yellowing streetlights. She can see herself lying on the slippery couch in a dirty tracksuit that's too small, and she's holding a screaming kid and an empty can of beer, and she knows this isn't any sort of a fairy tale. Or worse, maybe she's just got it backwards, and then no wonder it's all gone wrong, because perhaps Robbie's been rescued already. Who said she wasn't the witch all along?

She starts to cry then, and shoves Merlin back onto the couch because she can't bear to touch him, and then she's stumbling out of the room and snatching up her grubby plastic handbag. Tracey's done with her story; she's headed down the railway cutting or the wine bars or anywhere else that'll have her just as she is.

In the morning, she throws out the adult education brochures, drops them into the bin on top of the soiled nappies and solid chip fat. There aren't fairies any more, she thinks, not nowadays. And children aren't snatched away by the elves, and iron over the door won't keep out anyone worth their salt. Tracey loves Merlin, but she doesn't think it matters now. They'll take him sooner or later, just like Robbie, the fairies and the princes and the witches with their Colgate smiles. She doesn't even bother writing his name in the record book.

She'll look for Merlin and Robbie, though. She'll look for them for more than fifty years. She'll glance in prams lined up outside the supermarket and peer into thorn thickets by the railway. She'll look in the cafes in Swansea and the newspaper photos of A-level kids, in the disused mineshafts and the wedding announcements in the *Western Mail*. She'll keep watch all her life, while the nights fall and the years rush past, while the foxgloves shake and she slowly grows old.

I See You in Triplicate

A lot of things have gone missing, lately.

The apples Caroline bought last week, for example, and her favourite necklace, and the leaves that used to be on the sycamore across the road, and her husband, and one of the pink-and-white-striped gym socks from Woolworths.

Of these: the apples have all been gnawed away during the recent tearful nights, and their sinews cluster like mice on her bedside table; the necklace is tangled in a blue silk scarf that used to be her mother's; the gym sock is somewhere in the sliding layers of her knickers drawer; the sycamore leaves are composting on the ground; and her husband is in the water heater.

"It's been making these noises, you see," she explains. "My husband – my ex-husband – flushed it out, and it's never been right since."

Alex listens with his head on one side and a gentle, questioning smile. He would have made a good doctor; had always intended to be one, but when he was seventeen his mother died and he failed his A-levels. He's the first man Caroline has had in this bedroom – except, of course, for the husband now scratching away at the immersion heater – and his next appointment will turn out to be with Zinat, who has blue eyes and three children and a broken-down washing machine. Zinat smells of rosewater and Weetabix, her children are named after Afghan refugees and Alex will remember the braveness and blueness of her eyes for the rest of his life. He will not remember Caroline, even though the limescale remover he prescribes will dissolve her husband and leave her drifting through the quiet afternoon to cry, and shove her hand viciously into her jeans, and rasp her swollen thoughts up against firemen, or headmasters, or perhaps handsome young doctors named Alex.

Caroline's husband, though, doesn't stay gone. He knocks on the door at six the next evening, all buttoned and combed.

"Is this an okay time?" he asks. "Just to grab some… necessities?" and Caroline folds her arms, all *her* necessities ripped loose from their lodgements in her heart, and tells him he can have anything he fucking likes.

Ten minutes later he comes downstairs with a holdall crammed full of mistakes. He's taken his wedding suit – too tight now and punctured by moths – and left his jeans; he's taken the second book of The Raj Quartet and forgotten the first, which lies dusty on the spare-room shelves. He's jammed a sheaf of paper on top; this will turn out not to be the mortgage documents but rather Caroline's enrolment form for a Spanish evening class. It isn't his fault, this baffled, hurried packing like an Afghan refugee. The banging of the water heater has distracted him, and he wonders if he ought to get that fixed.

In the kitchen, meanwhile, Caroline is gnawing at the shining rind of a Granny Smith and drinking gin from a jar that once held his home-made chutney. The apple peel has the nutrients, her mother used to say; the peel makes your hair curl, and your nails shine, and spells out your husband's name on Midsummer Night. But Caroline's hair and nails are limp, her nutrients lately come from takeaway dinners and candy-coloured multivitamins, and she has just spent a considerable sum of money to dissolve her husband only to have him skulk up to the door the very next day. She has had quite enough of apple peel.

"Right. Well, I've got this lot, so..." He holds the bag up, awkwardly, and makes a pantomime little grimace to show how heavy it is. "Shall I be off, then?"

Caroline doesn't answer. He will be off, whatever she says, to that other woman; to a dinner packed with nutrients and perhaps even a nursery pudding to follow. Her husband has told her this woman has a child, as though that might make things better, or perhaps worse.

The front door clicks shut. He's gone, then – again – and the world hasn't fallen in, and she's still sitting in her kitchen with her apples and gin. She pours herself a complacent second measure for standing it all, for *bearing up so well*, and then she hears the snap of the letterbox as her husband finds out the least important of his mistakes and pushes her Spanish enrolment forms through. The chutney jar shivers into fragments under her fingers and the second measure becomes a third, and a fourth, and then she is not bearing up at all.

Caroline's second bag of apples is now half-finished, the sycamore tree is a naked shock against the muddy sky, her gym sock is draped stiff and mateless over the clothes horse, and her husband is in her Spanish enrolment forms. When she'd picked them up from the doormat she'd remembered how he filled them in for her last summer when she sprained her wrist, before the other woman and the water heater, before Zinat's washing machine broke down and Alex fell in love, before Afghan refugees and apples and gin.

Her husband winks at her from the pen strokes, tugging at the curl of her name and squatting cross-legged in the letters of what used to be their shared address. He always had lovely handwriting; had wanted to be an artist but at seventeen his best friend failed his A-levels when his mother died, and Caroline's husband decided to be a doctor instead. Caroline thinks about crumpling him up, dropping him on top of the drying teabags in the kitchen bin, but she doesn't feel quite up to that. In the end she stuffs him into an envelope and takes him to the post office, where he'll become Royal Mail's problem. She buys a stamp from the woman behind the till, a girl with brave blue eyes and a faintly soiled white blouse. Her nametag says Zinat; she's flicking through her phone in search of a plumber because she can't, she really can't, go another day without doing laundry, and Caroline forgets her instantly.

The Spanish class begins a week later. Caroline's been told to bring a photocopy of her forms, but she imagines her husband duplicated, triplicated, whirred into infinity by the forgettable post office girl, and firmly shakes her head.

That evening she sits in a bright classroom full of half-size chairs and finger-painted eggshells. It smells of chalk-and-school-shoes and gentle childhood bullying, and when Caroline is given a single flashcard with *Yo Soy* – I Am – on it, she almost bursts into tears from the simplicity of it all.

After that she learns *Las manzanas son mi comida favorita* – apples are my favourite food – and this too makes her cry, because it reminds her that her husband, who is not hers any more, is at that moment packing yet another bag in the house that is not theirs any more. Her conversation partner, a stocky woman with skin like sponge cake, leans over and pats Caroline's arm.

"Are you okay, love?"

It's so casual, that *love*, but Caroline is more grateful for it than she can possibly say and so instead she asks, extremely politely, what the woman's favourite colour is.

"¿Cuál es tu color favorito?"

When class is over there's a shuffling of papers, a stamping of boots, and winding of scarves. Some women have already paired off, leaving arm in arm in a kind of belted, middle-class companionship. The men are more circumspect, ducking their heads with a tender shame as they scamper off into the night.

"Hang on, pet." The sponge-cake woman's name is Ros, and for class she's been given the Spanish name Rosa. Caroline likes Ros, but she isn't sure about Rosa, who has far less to say for herself. Ros crooks an arm for Caroline to take, and in that nuzzling bump of elbows Caroline can see a friendship; she can see them growing old together disreputably; she can see stout-and-milks and knitted M&S jumpers and cackling, bawdy laughter as they pass blushing young doctors named Alex. This is not quite what she'd been expecting, but she knows this woman's favourite colour, she knows her favourite food, and at the next lesson she will learn how many brothers she has, and from there to the stout-and-milks seems hardly a stretch at all.

A month later, Caroline's husband comes back again. He brings a carful of empty boxes this time, and a list on his mistress's green notepaper. She's even printed out a set of little checkboxes for him to tick off each item, and Caroline thinks briefly that it is by these measures that wars and heartbreak are averted, that Afghan refugees are saved and Spanish conjugations learnt. She has never, after all, been truly in the game.

"Will be you all right?" he asks, coming into the kitchen under his strange new hairstyle. He wants her to say no; he is already beginning to regret the mistress and the awful, innocent demands of her child. He would like to stay here, to make another jar of the chutney Caroline used to like, perhaps even to fix something around the house with competent masculine strength. But the chutney jars have all been smashed, the water heater is quiet for once, and Caroline is busy beating sponge cake and smiling down at its pockmarked skin. So instead he goes back to his mistress, to be checked off her lists and hung up in her kitchen with the dinner menus, where he will dangle uselessly for several years until one day, to his surprise, he will realise that he has turned out to be happy after all.

Caroline, too, is learning about happiness. Ros now comes to her house after class, and on occasion has even stayed the night amongst the Christmas decorations and lonely books that shiver on the spare-room shelves. She once left a pair of pink-and-white gym socks, and these have become so mixed up with the rest of the laundry that Caroline no longer remembers one was ever missing.

Ros hasn't fixed everything, but that would be too much to expect. She's sorted out the water heater; took a spanner to it the first night she stayed, and now the limescale has gone for good. But she hasn't stuck the sycamore leaves back on, nor has she un-shattered the jar that once held chutney, and still, on bad days, holds gin. Caroline's husband is still there occasionally, glittering out at her from the oddest corners. He pops up in the bathroom so often that one day she howls her way through a proper spring-clean and only then does he turn back into a half-finished pot of shaving cream and a splaying toothbrush.

Ros, sitting in the kitchen with her stout-and-milk, shakes her head. She is canny, Ros, and sees that soon Caroline will no longer need the bawdy elbow-crook of their friendship. She has a little cry over this, for Ros has a story too, had a husband and a plumber and a bravely blue-eyed son of her own, and would have liked them to come into it somehow. But she knows that Caroline isn't forever, and because of this, Ros has never invited her home. When everything's been sorted out, when everybody's been ticked off into their checkboxes and refugee camps and evening classes, she has no intention of finding Caroline in her water heater.

And then it's spring and – the taste for sponge cake having entirely left her – Caroline is again sitting at her kitchen table and peeling an apple. Ros has long gone, and by now is fast friends with the blue-eyed post office girl, whose Afghan-named children have lately been drifting, with flower-like mouths, into bad company.

Caroline is, to a certain extent, happy again. Her husband no longer peeps out from odd corners and she can go days without *bearing up*. She still goes to the Spanish class but, owing to a computer mix-up and her failure to produce photocopies of her enrolment form, has had to begin again at the same level. *Yo Soy*, she says, again and again, and one day soon a fair-haired young man will join the class. His favourite colour will be red, and his favourite food will be cheese, and afterwards he will ask her for a drink and scamper off into the night with her tucked firmly into the crook of his arm.

Caroline may one day marry this man and have a child with blue eyes and immense courage, like most young babies. When asked for his name, perhaps from somewhere in her bruised and dazzling mind, Caroline will fish out *Alex*.

Should something momentous happen during Alex's A-levels, he may put his plans to be a doctor aside and travel instead. Perhaps he'll get as far as Spain, where, having never learnt *Yo Soy*, he'll lose himself completely until he meets a blue-eyed Afghan refugee who smells of rosewater and sponge cake. She may be training to be a chef, and may even make him chutney in Baltic stained-glass jam pots and, later, when everyone has left everyone else for the last and final time, Alex will always be able to find her somewhere at the bottom of those tiny jars.

Peacocks

When I was small, nothing upset my grandmother. Lost shoes, lost homework, lost tempers; she sat calmly through it all and rocked and certainly didn't see what the fuss was about. *She'd* never lost a thing in her life.

She didn't have much to lose, of course, just one pair of ruby earrings and some white cotton saris that she stretched out to dry from a string across the bathroom. When I was tiny she would scoop me damp and soapy from the bath each night, resting me on her hip as her one gold tooth crunched down on some cloves. Together we'd watch streetlights crackle through the frosted glass and we'd pick at paint bubbles around the rackety sash window. The street curved away beneath us, mapped by swerving dabs of cigarettes and fluorescent bus shelters.

"I haven't lost anything, Asha," Ammuma would whisper as my skin began to chill into gooseflesh. "I've left it behind, that's all."

"Amma!"

It was black outside, and a gritty dawn banged its teeth against the windows. Through my bedroom doorway I could see the hall clock looming solid and certain; six o'clock exactly, with a make-no-mistake air about its hands.

It was my birthday, I was thirteen, and in the bathroom Ammuma was calling for her mother.

"Amma!"

I scrambled out of bed, peering over the splintered banisters. My mother was already swooping downstairs in her faded flannel nightgown. That was no surprise; she had eyes in her spectacles case and ears in her discarded slippers; she slept in catnaps and would shake me awake from nightmares before they'd even arrived. I saw her pause at the bathroom door and peer through the rainy drape of vests and tights. She reached up, sweeping all the clothes down into puddles on the floor. I could see Ammuma then, leaning over the greenish sink with a single red earring glinting in the nest of her hair. She looked confused, with a misery that deepened at the sight of my mother's sleepless eyes and lemon-juice mouth.

Ammuma had come to live with us just after I'd turned three, after Dad had left for the last time. I remember the frost that edged up around the windows that morning, and the blurred smell of the iced-over grass and the way everything seemed to be holding its breath. At Heathrow I'd pulled my hand free and scuttled away to examine the people waiting by the arrivals barrier. At the front I'd seen an immaculate family: mother-father-son, with the father's arms folded over a portly stomach and the mother's eyes hidden safe behind sunglasses. At the back, my own mother had looked lost, alone with her naked eyes and their rags of worry.

As the arrivals gate opened, the portly father beamed, tucking his chin into his neck with a lordly welcome-to-you-all air. His cordial smile had run straight over the head of Ammuma, stumping past with the knotted limp of what would soon become full-blown arthritis. She was old, I remember thinking – impossibly, frighteningly old.

I remember how she'd turned to wink at me while my mother pressed her lips together and fumbled with the car-seat buckles. Mum only smelled of cheap peppermint shower gel, but Ammuma was spices and sandalwood, and she'd slipped a packet of boiled sweets bright as party-frocks into my fist. She'd yawned as we turned into our road with its canyon-walls of grey terraced houses, and I'd stared at her fascinating curd-soft chin, her gums packed tight with cloves. But it was that carelessly golden front tooth that had given her away, had made me rumble with joy and bang my feet until my mother had turned around at the red lights to slap my legs. Not that that had mattered, not in the slightest, because I'd found out my grandmother was a princess.

The curtains were pulled back when I woke again, letting in a shivering daylight. Outside I could see our greyish pocket of lawn licked with frost, and a cat blinking narrow eyes at me from the neighbour's roof.

My mother was downstairs, huddled into a cardigan and stirring a huge saucepan of porridge. She never made it the way Jess's mum did, or even the way the dinner-ladies did at school. Instead, she ladled in honey and raisins, coconut and cardamom and any spices she found to hand. After twenty years my mother was as English as could be, but she never quite believed in the food.

"Happy birthday, Anna!" There was a cupcake on my plate, one of the ones Mum had made after work last night. She'd spent an hour mixing the dough, the sleeves of her old dressing gown rolled back and her hair scraped into a pursed little bun. She never left her hair loose; even in bed my mother lay rammed full of pins and buttoned tight to the neck.

"It's *Asha*," I snapped. Last year Ammuma had been well enough to eat with us on my birthday. She'd given me a bracelet thin as a hair – real gold, she'd said it was, salt-bright and flaked with age. She'd sung Happy Birthday in Malayalam and told me about how wonderful it would have been back in India. *Jewels beside your plate, Asha. A tiger for a footstool and peacocks to sing you downstairs.* My mother had screwed her face up tight as steel wool and turned back to the stove. *Peacocks don't sing*, she'd muttered just under her breath.

"What happened to Ammuma last night?" I poked at the cupcake. She'd baked something into it, hidden under the icing. Dark lines of food colouring curled there, laced just like the henna in the wedding photos Mum still kept on her bedside table. I pushed the cake away.

"Anna…" She turned away, splashed a little in the empty washing-up bowl. When she turned around again, her smile was glued on, hooked right over her ears in a stretched, make-the-best-of-it way. My mother *always* made the best of it.

"She lost her earring when she got up to wash her face," Mum said eventually. "Before puja." That smile snagged a little on the last word; she didn't approve. Making puja was like tigers, was like princesses or peacocks or dads; there was no room for it in her house.

"Oh no, you should have come and got me. She'll need me –" I scraped my chair back, leaving thick black marks into the floor.

"It can wait, Anna." She was keeping her temper. "Why don't you open your present first?"

She slid an envelope onto the table to nudge against my fingers. It was a thin fold of airmail paper, the flimsy kind she used to write to Dad on. Inside was a cheque signed with a wavering sort of delicacy, as though my mother had had second thoughts.

To Anna Nair, pay £100 EXACTLY. NON-NEGOTIABLE.

The cheque was a month's worth of the groceries she brought home in cardboard boxes after the night shift at Iceland. It was six months of bus fares and Sunday trips to the zoo, it was Christmas and birthdays and Diwali all rolled in together. It was wonderful.

Except, just like her, it was exact and non-negotiable. It scolded me for snatching before I'd even stretched out my hand. I traced those words with the tip of my finger while she looked away, humped her shoulders and peered down the alley where rubbish leaked from the tower block bins.

"Thanks, Mum."

She turned back and smiled at me, a shaky, blurred sort of smile. I didn't call her Mum very much anymore, not since Ammuma had told me the word in India was *Amma*. My mother answered to it, but in a cold-water, shrivelled kind of voice, and before long I'd stopped calling her anything at all.

After Ammuma arrived, I'd followed her around tight as a shadow, three feet of chubby supervision at her meals and walks and daily puja. Ammuma couldn't eat beef, I'd informed my mother – screeched it from my cross-legged seat on the chilly stairs as she came in with her hands full of groceries. How dare my mother buy beef, didn't she know *real* Indians never ate it? My mother's smile had slunk away as I'd folded my arms on a final demand. Chicken, it would be, or nothing, and I'd glared until she set aside the package of discount hamburgers she always brought home as a Friday-night treat. In the morning it had still been there, melted into a shaming, sodden puddle on the kitchen table.

I'd coaxed Ammuma on her daily walk, shepherding her across the wasteland of scattered bricks and drying washing that hemmed in our terrace. We'd strutted past the smeared windows, two princesses tight together as fish in a tea-kettle. We'd walked over gutters stuffed with rubbish while she told me about wide, clean roads under purple jacaranda. She told me about palaces and magic, about Ravan and Rama and Sita, whom I secretly envied. And she'd told me about her wedding, with the carpet of marigolds so thick they'd had to float it down on a flat-bottomed riverboat. There'd been elephants too, draped in satin, and jewels – pounds and pounds of them – that lapped round her wrists and crusted at her throat.

She'd always stopped there, lost somewhere among the jewels and wedding sweets with a little sigh that shook it all back down inside herself. The end of our walk was along shabby grey streets, with nothing to look forward to but my mother's warmed-up smile from the scallop of the kitchen window.

By the time I'd finished breakfast it was overcast and everything was tinged with a sulky yellow-milk light. The hall was cold, and in the kitchen I heard a sodden clatter as my mother began the washing-up.

Ammuma's door was open, with a slice of blanket tucked over the bed. My mother cleaned the bedrooms as soon as she got up, leaving them chilled and shadowless. A string of tarnished bells was draped over Ammuma's door, and when I came in they began to knock with a peevish rattle.

"Ammuma?" She was sitting in the sturdy hospital chair my mother had set in a corner. As she turned her head I could see a gleam of a single red stone in her ear. It gave her a lopsided, awkward look, like a bird caught by the leg.

"Amma said you lost your earring?"

She nodded, patted her lap for me to sit down. "Happy birthday, little one."

I twisted my fingers in the front of my top, crumpling the nylon as hard as I could.

"You mean – your wedding earring?"

She looked away when I said that, shifted in her chair as though something not-quite-right had crept in on my heels.

"But Ammuma! Amma said it didn't matter, she said –" I was angry, but it was a scabby sort of anger, cracked with guilt. Beneath it all, I was glad my mother hadn't understood.

"Oh, Asha, don't worry…" She touched my hair as I knelt down beside her, began to plait it the way she had when I was small and I'd clung to her with starfish fingers after my bath.

"I'll fix it for you, Ammuma," I whispered.

She didn't reply. When I closed my eyes, I could hear her breathe, shaky and small over the noise of my mother scrubbing plates in bone-cold water

"Come on, Jess!"

Jess had a round face blotched with red, and pale hair tied in thin rat-tail plaits. She was top of my class in school, she had riding lessons and jelly-glitter shoes, and on a good day we were best friends forever.

My mother liked Jess too, liked her polite smile and soapy pink-and-white manners. When she'd knocked on the door with a mouthful of Good-morning-Mrs-Nair to invite me out shopping, my mother hadn't even thought twice.

"Goodbye, Mrs Nair," Jess called as we left, and I made a face at her. Her mother was waiting in the car for us, a smile tucked in at the edges of her round blue eyes.

When we got to the shopping centre, Jess wouldn't come to the bank. She shook her head, snuffling and staring furiously at a window that held nothing more exciting than discounted kettles. When I came back after cashing the cheque, she tucked her bottom lip in and put her hands behind her back, as though if she were good enough then I wouldn't rub off.

The Swarovski shop was by the far wall, a grotto of glass where pallid rainbows shifted and swam. Jess loved that shop, monkeying her fingers over the display cabinets and sighing damply with longing.

"They're all so *pretty*," she breathed. The assistant glanced over, lacquered smooth in her pencil skirt and high heels, and Jess snatched her hand back. "But does your granny really wear stuff like this? Mine only wants, like, hand cream. Or talcum powder."

I'd met Jess's grandmother once, a placid dumpling of a woman with wrinkles puffed out by fat.

"Yeah, she really does, Jess. Back in India she was a princess. I told you."

Jess looked doubtful, her mouth hanging open again with that anxious snuffle. I heard her wander away, then suck her breath in with a dramatic gasp.

"Anna, *look*!" She was pointing at something at the very back of the counter, a glittering scrunch of rubies and glass.

"It's a little expensive, girls." The assistant slid in front of us, a fluid stripe of tobacco-coloured hair and exaggerated nails. "Ninety pounds."

I set my teeth and felt the money, greasy in my pocket. "I'd like to buy it, please."

She seemed to take an age to wrap it, packing a sheeny box with tissue paper and no room for regret. I turned to Jess and smiled.

"She'll love it, Jess." That sounded brave even to me, with a bright, grown-up kind of ring. But Jess's face was a round moon of I-didn't-think-you-meant-it dismay, eyes wide under those watery lights. She shuffled towards the door while I paid, with her eyes fixed down on her jelly-glitter shoes.

Her mother was waiting for us across the food court, nestled in among its plastic tables and sticky trays. She waved, with a smile for Jess that seemed to spring up through the grain of her face. But then she saw the jewellery box and something changed; a pinch of caution biting at the edge of her smile.

"Lovely, dear. Your gran's going to be on top of the world."

But Jess, clever Jess, with her careful manners, shrank back against the table and wouldn't raise her eyes. When we got in the car I heard her hiss to her mother, *It was almost a hundred pounds!* in a breathy, horrified whisper. She clapped her hand over her mouth as soon as she'd said it, tucked her lip good-girl neat behind her teeth again and turned to stare through the window at the tepid, late-afternoon clouds.

When we stopped in the tiny space outside my house she clutched my hand. The oily shine on her face under the streetlights looked like tears.

"Happy birthday, Anna," and for a heartbeat we were friends again.

The house was dark when I pushed the door open, with an acrid smell creeping from the electric heaters. My mother never switched them on before the evening, and a faint line of frost edged the hallway windows. A warm, wet streak of light furled out from Ammuma's room, where she sat still and watchful, her hair washed and dripping onto a towel over her shoulders.

"Ammuma!" I whispered, and she nodded a little, her eyes bleary till they settled on me. Her sari was damp with my mother's palm-prints and trailed on the floor where a knot had come untucked.

I wish she'd just wear a skirt, my mother had muttered one day, in the middle of folding and ironing those yards of cotton. But I hadn't ever thought she'd do this, saunter off to work and leave Ammuma in a half-knotted sari and wrung-out hair. I slammed the door open and snatched up an armful of the loose cloth, bundling it up into Ammuma's lap.

"I can't believe her! I hate her. She won't even tie your sari. I hate her, I hate her…" I gave a heave on the fabric, trying to gather it up in the elegant, tucked way my mother tied it every day. But the folds began to unravel and when I grabbed at them they tangled, falling away from her lap in a wrinkled heap.

"Asha, stop. Stop. It's okay. It's okay." Ammuma pushed at me a little with her paper-dry palm, the bones so delicate they jostled under her skin. She'd started to shiver, with the sari lumped around her sides.

"Amma –" the cold tap in the bathroom began to spit and then the door swung open. My mother was in there, had been there all along wiping down the bath with its greenish rust. I saw her pick up the flannel and come out, barefoot with her skirt tucked up round her waist. It was the first time I had ever seen her hair loose, and it tongued down in wet ringlets. She even moved in a different way, with a lovely knock and sway in her hips and a comfort in her arms. She was talking as she came in, a liquid curl of words in a language I didn't know.

"Anna!" When she saw me her smile locked, settling taut and wedged beneath her cheekbones. "Did you have a good time, love?"

She turned to set the wash flannel down and saw the jewellery bag that I'd dropped in the doorway. The earrings had tumbled out, and under the dim ceiling light they looked gaudier than before: cheap red stones surrounded by Barbie-pink sparkles.

"Anna? Did you buy these?" Her voice was bright, but underneath it I heard that same breathy, hissed dismay as Jess's.

"They're for Ammuma," I began. "Because she lost her wedding jewellery, and –" And a lot of things, I wanted to say. And she used to hold me on her lap and tell me about the peacocks singing, and because nobody else – not even Jess, with her jelly-glitter sandals – has a princess for a grandmother, and because I never learnt to tie a sari, and my birthday present was exact and non-negotiable and came in one of those stupid airmail envelopes that Dad had never even answered, not ever, and –

"And I never even knew you *spoke* Malayalam," I burst out, and watched my mother's smile fade.

Three hours later my curtains were drawn, and I had scuffled the blankets up on my bed to make a musty cave. The house was quiet, creaking its way into the night, when a light snapped on in my mother's room. It was just bright enough to see the outline of my window, and a moment later my mother eased the door open. Her hair was tied up again, but her feet were still bare and her calloused heels caught on the stiff carpet.

"Anna?" I felt the bed sink as she sat down. "I'm sorry about today. It was lovely of you to buy something for

Ammuma." I didn't answer, and for a while we were quiet, breathing in the used-up air.

"Anna, you do know Ammuma was just telling you stories, don't you, about India? The palaces and the princesses and everything?"

I didn't answer.

"It's –" She paused and then gave a sigh, a little shake just like Ammuma when she talked about her wedding. "It was just like here."

I thought about *here*, about the gust and spit of wind as litter blew along the street, about the shrill white glare of the twenty-four-hour Iceland, about the cold, dusty smell of the electric heaters and that look on Jess's face, and the way Mum could still draw the henna patterns in her wedding photograph even after twenty years.

She stood up, and I could hear she was pulling herself together, making the best of it. When she left I dragged the covers back over my head, but her light stayed on all night, and every time I woke I could see its glow at the edge of my window. Somewhere in that room she was coming to terms with it all, folding up saris and filing cupcake recipes, leaving nothing behind but the spaces where things had been tidied away.

Daylight Savings

At just past two in the morning Sarah switches off her alarm, buttons her dressing gown, and sits down to write to Amber's husband. This isn't, she understands, quite a normal thing to do. It's less normal, say, than going for after-work drinks. It's less normal than wearing M&S knickers and standing in bus queues and tracking the FTSE index, all of which she does quite regularly. She has an excuse, though. This is not exactly a normal night.

She takes a biscuit from the pack on her desk and sucks at the chocolate coating. Tonight is the end of daylight savings, and she's riding on the back of a night-time stammer, an hour when the clocks go back and nothing counts, not biscuits nor diets – nor adultery, she thinks with determination, and applies herself to the task of telling Colin exactly what she's wearing.

"A rose-patterned chemise, love," she writes. "And those silky stockings you bought me." She touches the knot of her flannel dressing gown, slipping her fingers inside. It's a lie, but it won't last long. In twenty minutes her extra hour will be over, and then she'll happily admit to wearing her comfortable old nightgown. A few more minutes and she'll even confess that Colin hasn't, in fact, bought her any stockings. And not long after that, the final truth. He isn't, in any way, her lover.

She nibbles at the corner of another biscuit and contemplates toast. She hasn't quite finished her letter, but she still heaves herself out of the chair and pads down the sea-green gloom to her kitchen. In a horror film this is the point where she'd be found, where she'd be ravished while the camera lingered on that wonderful chemise. She looks about the kitchen hopefully, but Sarah has never been the kind to be found. Not by the right person anyway. She carves herself a ragged slice off a white loaf.

Colin spends most of the year consigned to a blurred stack of photographs tucked into her university leavers' book. She remembers the photographs at odd intervals but has long since forgotten the events. Punting in summer, and Colin's hand inching up underneath her shirt. When his fingers encounter the roll of her stomach he will flinch, beat a hasty retreat. Sticky skin against hers under the thin sheets of his bed in halls, her back to the cold brick wall separating them from next door's showers and the groans of splashing students. Awkward silences in the pub, her wrists clammy from resting on beermats sodden with someone else's happiness. No, she decides. She doesn't remember those things.

They'd broken up one night in September after an anaemic fight, a bloodless battle dangling limply from *ifs* and *buts* and *it's for the bests*. She could take a hint, she'd told him with dignity, she wasn't the sort to go where she wasn't wanted. Ten years later, Sarah finds this bewildering. She must have thought it was a virtue, at the time.

Colin had been pleased, relief shining from his freckles and his gangly limbs twitching with *I told you so*.

"So that's it then," he'd said, triumphantly. At that moment his golden hair had begun to fade, dimming to an unappealing mouse-brown. He'd offered to walk her to the bus stop, where she'd stood with chilled feet and bruised dignity until it became clear the last bus had gone. She trailed three paces behind him – and had he always been so skinny? Had he always had dandruff? – back to his hygienic room in halls.

She remembers what followed, the glowing numbers on his alarm clock rolling back as her fingers scuttled under the blankets. Daylight savings. A hiccup, a scratched record, a chance to make the same mistakes twice. An hour that didn't count; an hour for Colin to reclaim his gorgeous, golden-brown beauty. He hadn't, though. He'd plucked himself free after a single aching minute. She had no sense, he'd informed her, of the decencies.

He'd gone on to date and marry Amber, two years younger than Sarah and sopped through and through with decency. By then, to Sarah, his hair was definitely brown and his teeth a filmy yellow. And that's how he stayed for almost ten years, installed in a Croydon semi-detached with Amber by his side. But once a year, when the clocks go back, she still writes to him. It's her private hour, sixty stolen minutes when he's beautiful again, when he rolls naked under her pen and sprawls across her desk.

She swallows the last of the cocoa, stows the mug and glances at the clock. It's all over now, and she wishes Amber joy of him.

The next morning, Sarah adds one more page to the small stack of letters in her desk. Last night's words catch her eye. *A rose-patterned chemise, love.* She's never sent any of the letters. They aren't for Colin, not the real Colin with his thinning hair and golf-buggy paunch, with his normal wife and normal baby and his almost-certainly-normal decencies.

Sarah slips off her dressing gown in the bedroom, bleached by morning light. A mirror hangs on the back of the door, with another propped beside it on the dressing table. Mirror-Sarah looks back at her, slab-pale, jellied with fat and swags of flesh. Before Sarah turns away, she gives her mirror-self a slick of make-up, a tighter waist, a rose-patterned chemise. They don't suit her.

Sarah looks away as she pulls on her trousers. She makes sure her desk is clear and all the toast crumbs brushed away. Amber's coming to visit this afternoon, and Sarah – snuffling around her house, padding through rooms and nosing at smells – is covering her tracks.

In her gloss-emulsion bedroom in Croydon, Amber pulls out a pair of ballet flats and fluffs the dust from the diamante buckles. Her feet are still swollen and the shoes too tight, but she wants to dress up. She prods at her lipstick, edges it with careful liner, but it makes no difference. The paint's feathering, bleeding into cracks in much the same way that everything else is for Amber these days.

She's off to see Sarah, though, which always cheers her up. Sarah – poor Sarah, she qualifies kindly – used to pal around with Colin at university, long before Amber knew either of them. Amber's kept in touch with Sarah; she's sent pre-printed Hallmark cards at Christmas and offered to introduce her to some really *nice* men. Divorced, but you can't be too choosy, she thinks. Not when you're Sarah.

Amber lives on a raw-boned estate new as an egg, and today she's taking Poppy out for the first time. Poppy's two months old and Amber's still not sure what to make of her. She picks the baby up, adjusts her pink ribbons and settles the damp weight onto her hip. Amber doesn't have many achievements but – unlike poor Sarah – she hasn't made many mistakes either. Poppy, at this stage, could turn out to be either.

"Amber, how nice to see you." Sarah pulls the door wider. Amber still hasn't quite lost the baby weight, looks older and more formidable in those silly shoes of hers. Diamante, thinks Sarah. *Honestly.*

"Sarah, darling, you look wonderful!" Amber kisses Sarah twice, once on each meaty cheek. She's charming, thinks Sarah, who isn't. Sarah accepts the pecks, but mistrusts charm.

"And Poppy, too. How lovely to meet her." Sarah takes them through to the living room, where she's set out plates of cakes iced in lurid pink. The room's reflected in two mirrors, giant ones that came with the house and which Sarah's never dared to remove. For someone of her size, throwing out mirrors can hardly be a neutral act. She'd be taking a side, taking up arms against mirror-Sarah, and she isn't at all sure who would win. Instead, she narrows her eyes at the glass as a multitude of Ambers beam simultaneously down.

"It was wonderful, Sarah. The birth, I mean. Almost orgasmic, and I was in the birthing pool and just felt so… so nurturing, and –" Amber, nipping at frosting and dabbing her lipstick, launches herself on a description. Sarah listens with polite interest. She's not the sort of person to whom these things would happen.

"And how's Colin?" Sarah asks eventually. By now they've exhausted childbirth, Amber's maternal instincts and her sore nipples and her five stitches which tore right through. Where else is there to go?

Amber tucks her legs up and leans closer in a waft of perfume and baby powder. "Well, it's hard for men at first, isn't it? Adjusting."

Colin has been distant since Poppy's birth, and Amber wants to complain. She wants to luxuriate in feminine woe and to make those slightly bitter, wry observations about men which she thinks would be appropriate. She'd like Sarah to tell her she doesn't need a man, an observation she plans to cap indulgently by noting that she seems to be stuck with one. Sarah, however, does nothing of the sort.

"I suppose so." Sarah leans forward, picks at a cake and puts it back. Amber's reflection, looking down on her, nods in approval.

Sarah's done well, thinks Amber. She's dieting and denying herself; she's *getting there*. Yes, Amber thinks. If Sarah lost some weight, if she smartened herself up… perhaps a really *nice* divorced man. She feels almost fondly towards Sarah right now. Confessional, in a way.

"Last night, though… well, that was different." Amber smiles. She means to be kind; she means to confide.

"I gave Poppy a bottle about two. And then Colin said we had an extra hour, so" – she licks her lips, pulpy as oysters, and Sarah thinks briefly of her own extra hour, of gold and roses and lovers at dawn – "we were at it for an hour." She finishes with a giggle. "I didn't think he could keep it up."

Sarah feels a lurch, a jab of malice that whips down her spine and coils out to those diamante flats. Amber has just appropriated her hour, has climbed right into it with a baby and a milk bottle and a husband she can fuck without even losing sleep. And that husband is Colin, and if Sarah thinks too hard about *that* then she knows her own rose-and-gold lover will vanish, will climb unceremoniously out the window and leave nothing but dank sheets and white-brick walls and an alarm clock ringing out her mistakes. She is dimly aware of betrayal, and of Poppy beginning to cry.

Amber bends over her daughter, pulling her top down so that Poppy can suck. Sarah's mirrors obligingly reflect her: Madonna and child. And mirror-Sarah, too, sitting lumpish and charmless by herself without even a rose-patterned chemise for comfort. She should have stuck with the M&S knickers, she thinks, with the toast and the FTSE index and the virtues of going where she's wanted.

"And what about you?" Amber tucks a neat breast back into her top. These are the rules; Sarah has to confess, too. "What's the gossip?"

Sarah, with nothing to confess, resents the question. She's under a lot of stress that afternoon, what with Colin's wife and his baby and his unexpectedly fulfilling sex life, and so she feels she has some excuse, at least, for what happens next.

"I've been seeing someone, too. An old flame from university." Mirror-Sarah grins at these words. Like everything in a mirror, she can't quite be trusted, and is egging Sarah on disgracefully.

"Oh, but Sarah!" Amber, ensconced on the sofa with knees together and Poppy slipping like a battered handbag to the floor, gives a delicious little giggle. "Who is it? Anybody I'd know?"

This, as Sarah will determine later, is where she makes a mistake. It's true that malice is still churning inside her, and true that Amber is insufferable and true that it is, after all, an unseasonably hot afternoon and tempers are frayed. But nonetheless, as she will later conclude, she makes a mistake.

"Oh, no," she says. "He's quite before your time." She gets to her solid feet and crosses the room to her desk. "He's been sending me letters."

Amber smiles. "Oh, look at *you*," she coos. Letters, she thinks. How appropriate, how perfect. She can think of nothing better – for Sarah. "What does he say?" she asks with a savage kind of curiosity.

So much, Sarah thinks, for the decencies. She wonders if Colin knows what he's married, and decides that he probably does. She takes up one of the sheets of paper and begins to read.

"I miss you so much tonight, Sarah. I miss licking your lips before we kiss." She looks up, notes a gleam of memory flash over Amber's face.

"I miss our nights in halls, that second-floor room next to the showers."

Amber's face is puzzled. She knows the halls; she lived there for three years herself. There was only one room next to the showers, as Amber knows very well. White-brick walls, hygienic, with Colin's alarm clock rolling back just as it ought. No trace left of Sarah under those thin sheets, not by the time Amber came along.

"I miss you pulling my hair," Sarah continues. "Rough. The way I like it. The way wives don't do."

It's a gamble, that last line. For all she knows, wives do. Judging by Amber, wives are the vicious sort. The sort who might very well indulge in hair-pulling, in little pinches and slaps. Sarah wouldn't put anything past them.

But Amber's smile is collapsing. She's floundering to her feet, a dark red flush mottling her pretty face and smearing her lipstick.

Amber is full of suspicions and swollen, tender thoughts edged with jealousy. She tumbles Poppy into her arms with a defensive, protective shrug. She won't expose her child to Sarah's mind, to those... to those *obscenities*, Amber thinks indignantly. She doesn't ask to see Sarah again, or offer her cheek for a goodbye kiss.

And that night, too, Amber has a row with Colin.

"Writing letters?" he says. "To Sarah? Don't be ridiculous." There's an uncomfortable pause as the baby monitor begins to wail.

"But she was so... so gloating," Amber bleats. "And all the things she said... such things." Things which Amber wouldn't dream of discussing, herself.

"Look, can't you do something with Poppy?" Colin asks. The howling from the baby monitor is giving him a headache; Amber's getting on his nerves, and, quite frankly, he thinks as he watches his wife climb the stairs, he wouldn't mind having *had* this damn affair. Not with Sarah, of course. Never with Sarah.

Meanwhile, Sarah is climbing her own stairs, on a fruitless hunt for cocoa, or biscuits, or anything that will distract her. She's been sitting at her desk since Amber left, watching the afternoon fade and chewing on slices of toast. Everything's been fine, while the light lasted. But by evening, something is badly wrong.

Every time she passes a mirror, someone lurks behind mirror-Sarah, just out of sight. He's mouse-brown and short-sighted, he wears M&S underpants, he has a paunch and a bald spot and an entirely unsuitable wife. And although Sarah hasn't yet realised this, he will never leave.

From now on she'll spend that extra hour each autumn sleeping or eating or watching pale shadows in the dark, until fifty years later her sister will visit her in the hospice and dreamily add a touch of lipstick to that champing mouth that won't stop asking – will never stop asking until she dies five days later – for a rose-patterned chemise.

Farne Islands

It wasn't turning out at all like the guidebooks. Catherine wouldn't say so, though, not for worlds. Not when Emily had packed a bag full of old travel guides and she'd been sending away specially for tourist pamphlets for almost six weeks. Emily thumbed the pages each night in their hotel room with a muslin cap over her hair and her face cold-creamed. Catherine didn't bother with the cream and cap nowadays, and not very much with the guidebooks either.

"I think it helps," Emily had explained. "Planning things again." She'd piled the books up next to her hairpins and perfume bottles. "Mrs Smythe's paraphernalia", the hotel manager called the pile, with a sneering pity. Some of the travel guides were out of date, Catherine noticed. It didn't seem to matter.

"Not our best day." Emily's face was pinched with disappointment. It wasn't just the rain, Catherine knew. It was the hotel dining room, full of dusty tables and cracked teacups. It was the bored waitress. It was their quarrelsome and fragile afternoon and, at the end of it all, it was Tim's unrelenting absence. But so is *my* husband gone too, thought Catherine, and – with a sudden childish stab of unfairness – he's been dead longer than Tim.

"Let's have tea, dear," she soothed Emily, and began the hopeless task of trying to get it. It was their last evening and there was an end-of-things look about the hotel, with greenery dimming the windows and blurring the sepia photographs on the wall. Those weak-tea smiles reminded Catherine of the scrapbooks she and Tim had once played with in their grandmother's attic. As though they'd been important, once.

"The harbour," Emily read from the most optimistic of her guidebooks, "affords a fine view of the Farne Islands."

The hotel manager had mentioned that, too, when Catherine booked. But he wouldn't recommend the boat, he'd added with a jolly little chuckle, not if she and her sister-in-law weren't so steady on their feet. And Catherine had stared at Emily's brochures, with their cycle routes and boat trips all strung out like snapped threads, and agreed politely. No, she'd said. They weren't too steady on their feet.

But since today was their last day, they'd climbed down to the harbour anyway, where the Farne Islands lurked unseen behind a bank of fog. The pier was deserted, and fairy lights sagged above the queasy suck of waves.

"Tim would have loved this." Emily was limp with sadness, and Catherine – who, after all, had built sandcastles with Tim, had braved the tangling seaweed to bring him tidepool anemones – had to fight back an urge to slap her face.

"Come on, dear," she'd said instead, and shepherded Emily back to the hotel. They'd had lunch in the conservatory, stuffy with the smell of boiled beef and rain. Every time the door opened it let in a rattling blast of wind, and Emily blotted tears from her cheeks with a paper napkin. Catherine ordered them sandwiches and pressed her arm against Emily's shivering elbow and thought, no, it isn't like the guidebooks at all.

"Catherine, do catch her eye," Emily insisted, glaring at the waitress lolling against the far wall and picking at her nails. But just as Catherine looked up she heard the front door slam and voices spill in from the hall. The somnolent waitress perked up and hurried to fetch menus, her rump clucking under a tight black skirt. Emily brightened a little and closed her book with a snap that was almost decisive.

"After all, it's too dim to see, really," she explained to Catherine, and dabbed at her lipstick. She detests these endless evenings, too, Catherine reflected. We have nothing to talk about but Tim, and she allows me a polite half-share in him. But I don't recognise her Tim at all, and then, too, she is sorry for me.

"Oh, Harry, what a sweet hotel." A woman's voice in the hall, shrill and over-excited. Almost tearful, Catherine thought, as if there hadn't been enough already.

"Yes, a table please," the voice went on. "Just the two of us. It's our – bridal supper." There was a pause, a little gasp, before she hurled herself on the last two words.

"A bridal supper?" Something wistful tugged at the corners of Emily's mouth as she leant to whisper to Catherine. "It was a wedding breakfast in our time."

Yes, thought Catherine, and ours was such a *long* time ago – and here come those tears – as Emily began to crumple her second napkin of the day.

The woman who appeared at the door was older than Catherine had expected, with her collarbone sharp above a low neckline and her ankles strapped bravely into stilettos. There was a suggestion of shininess about her; a rustle of edges that didn't quite meet and lace straining over the seams of a brand-new frock.

"Of course, it was just the registry office today." She laid a confiding hand on the waitress's arm. "We're having a *real* do later."

"A registry office," Emily whispered. "Oh, Catherine, do you remember…"

Catherine did. The polished wooden chairs, the officiant with her drapey, comfortable bosom, Emily's peach-satin bridesmaids looking out of place amongst the parking permits and community health notices. Tim hadn't wanted a church.

The man bobbed his head in a choky way as the waitress fussed with tablecloths. He seemed on the point of an apology, an explanation of something, but subsided instead behind the silver tea set.

"I couldn't eat a thing, I'm that excited." The woman's voice was pitched to carry, and Catherine gave Emily a hesitant smile. For Emily had had so much more: the peach satin, the wedding flowers Catherine had arranged as a surprise with her school friend Beth. Even Tim's extravagant champagne toasts – *To my dear, my heart, my wife.* So, Catherine prayed, let Emily be amused by this; let her forget her sadness and her memories and those bloody awful guidebooks for just long enough to cope with it all.

Across the room, the man was ordering two plates of toast – plain, no extras – while the woman patted her hair with conscious modesty. She had magnificent nails, Catherine noticed, audacious silver talons that clattered against the teacups. "Harry!" she exclaimed. "Look – I've still got confetti in my hair. I must look awful."

"She doesn't though," Emily's voice was breathy. "He mustn't say so – he *mustn't*."

"You're fine, love." The man's teeth champed as he swallowed tea. Dentures, thought Catherine with a rush of distaste – and ill-fitting ones at that. Emily breathed a gentle sigh and dabbed at her eyes.

"Catherine?" She touched Catherine's hand across the tablecloth. "Why don't we send them a glass of champagne, dear?"

"Oh, Emily, I don't think…" Catherine protested. Emily had always melted into ready tears at weddings; at christenings, too, and the readings at Easter. She-Who-Weeps, Tim had whispered once to Catherine after a Christmas service washed with Emily's sadness, and Catherine had let out an explosive, unhappy giggle. Unfair, she had thought even then, to take sides. And now, at the sight of Emily's carefully made-up, miserable face, she gave in. As it's your birthday, she used to say to the children. As it's our last evening; as you asked nicely; as Tim is dead and we are both unsteady on our feet and one day soon you will be nothing to anyone but Mrs Smythe and her paraphernalia.

The manager had been glancing at them through the open door all evening, like a headmaster supervising children too dull-witted to misbehave. As Catherine signalled, he hurried over to their table with a reassuring smile. He'll be patting our hands next, she thought.

"We'd like to send some champagne to the… the newly-weds over there." Emily's face was upturned – with a short-sighted smile, Catherine thought, a widow's smile. Harmless and delicate.

"How wonderful. Right away, madam." Of course he would approve, and Catherine surprised herself in a flicker of anger. Emily would forgive her for that, she knew. Emily always forgave people beautifully.

When he'd gone, Emily gave her a lovely, tearful glance. "Thank you, dear. The wedding day's too early" – and out came the napkin again – "to start making the best of things."

Or perhaps too late, Catherine thought, and squeezed Emily's hand.

The manager emerged from the kitchen with two glasses of straw-coloured wine, meagre bubbles crawling up their sides. "With the compliments of an admirer," he announced and the woman blushed and wriggled in her ample seat.

"Oh, but today was just the registry," she demurred, and beamed around the room.

How important it is to her, Catherine thought, that this should *not* be all there is to it – the rainy sunset, and the groom's ill-fitting teeth, and all these pensioners sitting across from each other like pairs of withered ghouls.

"He didn't say the champagne was from us," she objected, but Emily waved that away.

"Never mind, dear. A wedding day should be special, shouldn't it?" she said.

It should be, Catherine agreed, and shut her lips tight on anything else.

An hour later – after Emily had exhausted her guidebooks, after she'd served up the Farne Islands several times over, tepid with travel advice – Catherine called for the bill. Emily sat back, her slender legs crossed at the ankles and her hands in her lap. I couldn't sit like that, thought Catherine. My thighs would bulge out like that poor bride's and my shins would begin to hurt in those dainty shoes. Emily looked boneless, held together with hatpins and lace.

From the corner of her eye Catherine saw the wedding couple examining their own bill. They whispered together for a few seconds, her with little pleading hand gestures, him with a sturdy refusal to listen. He looked up and beckoned the waitress over with a snap of his fingers.

"Look at this. I knew it," he told her. There was a nasty satisfaction in his voice, as though he'd been waiting for something to go wrong. "I knew this would happen. That bloody champagne."

A rustle went through the dining room, glances exchanged and smiles tucked into cheeks. Even Emily looked up, and the crepe-lines of her elegant throat fluttered.

"I tell you, somebody sent it. I don't know who." The man's voice was getting louder, and he glared with soft-boiled eyes around the room. "I didn't order it and I'm not paying."

The waitress clicked her pen shut against the palm of her hand and shifted her weight. "I'm sorry, sir."

"You'll just have to find who it was. Ask them." He folded his arms, sitting back in the chair. A faint look of disbelief rose in his wife's eyes. Her shoulders hunched and great blotches began to redden her neck. She seemed to be looking for reassurance – in the teapot, perhaps, or the trolley or the smiling, indifferent photographs. The waitress strolled to a neighbouring table, indicating the couple with a flick of her pen.

"Did you buy them champagne?" she asked loudly.

Emily gasped. "Oh, Catherine – say something. How awful!"

It's a bill, Catherine thought, a mix-up with the bill and nothing to be upset about. Nothing's been ruined forever.

But Emily's agitation got into the air around her, fluttered her eyelids with panic.

"Excuse me," Catherine called out, feeling faintly ridiculous. She struggled to her feet, grappling with her coat as it tangled around the chair legs. Her sturdy shoes caught on the coat's hem and a giggle came from somewhere in a corner. Two widows, Catherine thought, trying to manage with little gifts and little treats – and oh, but nothing's ruined forever. Something like a sob snagged in her capable throat and she stumbled across the carpet.

"Excuse me… we sent the champagne." It took her an interminable minute to make the waitress hear.

"Thank you, madam." The waitress turned back to the couple with a little swing of her hips. "It'll be taken off your bill, sir."

He seemed to swell, nodding with plump satisfaction and setting the wattles of his neck swaying. His wife didn't look up. *It doesn't matter*, Catherine hoped she'd say, *this isn't the real do*, but instead she fixed the window with the wide-eyed stare and white pinched nostrils of a child trying not to cry.

Back at the table, Emily was poised in her perfect distress. She tucked Catherine's coat under the table and drew in an elegant, courageous breath. "Oh dear… and on her wedding day. Catherine, how in the world didn't you notice it wasn't on our bill?"

But you didn't look either, Catherine could have shouted at her. Because Emily never had looked. Because of dead husbands and brothers, because of the missing Farne

Islands and that greasy, guilty laughter at Christmas. Because Catherine had always been taking sides, ever since she'd seen Tim slip out of Beth's car two weeks before the wedding, his face rosy and smacked with happiness glaring as a sunburn. *Nothing happened*, he'd insisted to Catherine, and over the long, pale years she'd watched him twist like string and wished that something had.

"I'm sorry, dear," she murmured instead, and thought hard and brightly about details, about packing and timetables and fog rolling past the Farne Islands to a limitless sea.

Seascapes

It isn't until she gets to the bus stop that Deepa knows her feet are wrong. They're aching a little under the hem of her sari, but that's not it. Perhaps they're just tired; she's already trotted along miles of vinyl corridors behind the hospital tea trolley and trudged through the evening's drizzling rain. She sits down, shakes her legs, and reads the graffiti daubed on the concrete wall. *Alex Loves Sara*. She likes that, hopes he does, but perhaps Sara wrote it herself. It's been that sort of day.

She frowns at her feet again. They're throbbing and damp and somehow she thinks they shouldn't be here at all. They should be fins instead; green and scaled and shimmering, with a shiver of muscle running down to the tip. It's an old trick from her childhood, when she used to sit on the damp concrete outside the Marina swimming pool in Madras and pretend to be a makara. A sea monster. She used to go further, pretend she had the swirling peacock feathers, the doomed and tragic eyes. Not any more though; not here.

But for a second she feels just like a makara again, and she examines those sturdy ankles that swelled when Rahul was born and haven't really gone down since. She hadn't thought that sea monsters had feet, but perhaps it doesn't matter in the end, and so she picks up her shopping and climbs onto the waiting bus. In the distance the Tyne swirls in an eddy of turbid brown.

She remembers another river, diamond-bright as it bubbled over her toes. A stream, really, with a bed of stones polished to smooth curves. She remembers the hillside near Middlesbrough, sloping and littered with greyish flints, and the distant factory chimneys that puffed out clouds of pure white smoke. Sheep-white and grass-green and sky-blue, she remembers, and the sun beating down forever on the clover that stained her hands.

She shifts her grip on the string handles. She's got cod for Bill's dinner, and she thinks she could stretch it for two days with some dal. Bill's not too fond of dal though – calls it fancy foreign muck when he's down at the pub, but he's gentle too; he tries to make sure she doesn't hear.

They'd had dal that day too, dolloped into lukewarm plastic containers and squashed with the chapattis into her mother's leather bag. That bag had come across with them all from Madras the winter before – Amma and Appa, little Anil, Deepa, Karthika-chechi with her woollen cardigans. All of them left a bit battered; all of them frozen and brown in a grey-white city.

And on their very first family outing – and this was the point in the story where Amma's eyes widened and her voice dropped with a delicious swoop – Deepa had got lost, somewhere on that steep green hillside. It's part of the family folklore, like when Blackie ran away or when Anil was summonsed for cycling without a light.

"When we called to fetch her back, she was gone!"

The suspense didn't last long. She'd turned up half an hour later playing with flints and in a tantrum about being found at all. But Deepa knows there's another part to the story, broken off like a jagged tooth in the back of her mouth. There's a part of the story where she wades upstream to a rocky crevice covered in fairy-green moss. Hidden deep within the spongy softness she uncovers a cleft where the water springs fresh and bubbling, finds a cavern just behind it that teems with nymphs and sirens with fish's tails. She dives in through the stony lips; she's tossed by waves and ground against rocks until she emerges polished as flint and changed into something else entirely.

Bill's waiting at home when she arrives, sitting in his old brown armchair by the television. She keeps meaning to have the place redecorated, but you can't get that sort of flock paper nowadays, and plain paint reminds her of the slums.

"It's fish tonight, dear."

She struggles out of her coat, the solid shape of her hips and shoulders stretched into the cloth, and runs cold water over the greasy breakfast dishes. Bill *will* leave his plate on the table, egg drying out and toast crumbs down the front of his shirt. He's kind, though; she gives him his due even inside her head, as the gas fire starts to warm the chilly kitchen and the fish splutters in the frying pan.

She shuffles back through to the living room, where Bill's chisel and hook knife lie on the table next to a half-carved toy horse. Something for Katie, Rahul's first, and such a pretty, fair girl, but she's getting far too old for wooden toys. She hopes Bill won't mind. Since he retired from the carpentering he likes to keep his hand in with carving, but it's all Lego and Sindy dolls now, and to tell the truth he never really was that good. He was a practical carpenter, turning out solid objects that lasted. She's glad he's stopped, she thinks, stretching her toes inside her worn carpet slippers and wishing for fins. There are already too many things in this country that last.

"I can't even swim," she says abruptly.

"Eh? What's that, pet?" Bill leans forward and switches off the set, looking at her with puzzlement. She can smell the fish smoking away in the kitchen – it'll be burnt, but he'll chew through it manfully and never notice.

"I want to learn how to swim."

He eyes her warily, and she can see he's wondering if this is the change. She's too old for that though; went through it ten years ago and had the house turned upside down with her sweats like the monsoon.

"They have those aquarobics classes," he ventures. "Down at the baths." His eyes are bleary but he's trying to please her, and so she sniffles a few times and hurries back to the kitchen to sit with her dupatta pulled over her head and listen to the dinner burning.

It's raining the next day, a cold drizzle, and her fingers are numb as she moves about the kitchen straightening things up. It's her day off, and someone else will have to dole out the polystyrene cups of scalding tea and feel the edge of Annie Higgs' tongue. Annie's got cancer, lies drenched with pain on a crumpled pillow and calls her a Paki when it gets too bad, though Deepa's never been near Pakistan in her life. She says she's just waiting to die, but Deepa knows differently. She'll hang on a good few more years, long past the time when Deepa herself will slough her skin and swim off instead with a monster's tail polished bright as an iron lung.

Bill's in front of the television again, puffing out yellow fug from his pipe. She's been asking him to stop for years, but he likes the feel of the stem in his mouth, and anyway, he spends more time fiddling with it than smoking. She used to mind the circle of dusty grey around his armchair where the ash grinds into the carpet, but by now she's used to it. Occasionally she imagines coming back home one day by herself, turning the stiff key in the door, wearing her white sari for the first time since her wedding – Bill's mam insisted, said it was the proper colour for brides, and Deepa had practically grown up here anyway, it wasn't as though she was really *foreign* – and seeing that island of ash.

"I found you those swimming classes," Bill announces. He's been up since five; he doesn't sleep much anyway and he's pleased to have a reason to be up out of the roil and muddle of the tangled bed sheets. She frowns. She knows what she said last night, and it's true – she thought she was a makara, and it's not as though you can be changing much at her time of life, so she supposes that she still is – but she no longer thinks that swimming will get her anywhere.

"Three o'clock." He hands her a brochure that must have been sitting in the back of a drawer for months, along with a takeaway menu and a notice about council meetings. "Senior Citizens Aquarobics", it reads. It's bright and glossy, with a picture of some smiling, shining nymphs: senior citizens in bright pink bathing caps. They're poised on the side of an ominously blue pool. *Don't jump*, she thinks – thinks of lemmings and suicide pacts and village girls flinging themselves from mango trees with rope around their necks. "Classes at 3pm".

She examines the picture dubiously. Perhaps somewhere in that chemical blue there's a rent, a gap where she can slip through to the palm trees and storm-filled skies of Madras, but she doesn't think so. All those ladies look too solid for that. They look like they're built to last.

Nevertheless, she agrees to go and have a look. Do some shopping, have some tea in town before she comes back to make the jam roly-poly for tonight. Bill would like her out of the house for a while, she knows. His sports programme is on soon and she's been edgy, snapping at him and burning the fish last night, although he'd never dream of saying so.

She takes a small rucksack with her, takes one of Karthika-chechi's old cardigans and a book for the trip. The pamphlet Bill gave her has the route to the baths, but she doesn't need it. She's not going to town, to aquarobics and shopping and tea. She's going back to find those stones that cut like glass and that spring that bubbled out of the fresh-tasting earth. She's going to scatter everything to glory with a single flick of her peacock tail, breakfast plates and bathing caps and bunions and all. She's going back to Middlesbrough.

She thanks the bus driver as she clambers down at the station to catch the express. He's a young lad, with a shock of hair like Anil before he went into the navy and cut it short and got himself killed in that accident out in Australia.

"Middlesbrough" says the board on the next bay, and so she climbs onto the express bus and tugs her blouse down against the cold. She has no picnic this time, no dal in plastic containers, no cold chapattis to stick to her fingers, nothing but a cardigan and a cheap rucksack, and it worries her. This is a journey. She should have taken provisions.

A few more people shuffle on to the bus. It's half past two on a bright Tuesday afternoon, and that's a *definite* time, a time for appointments and grocery shopping and bank managers. It's a time to be jotted in a diary with a ballpoint pen, but these people don't seem to have any plans at all. She rummages in her rucksack as the bus rolls out and finds a barley sugar. She unwraps it, and then, sucking, drops the paper deliberately on the floor. It's her own form of graffiti – *Deepa was here* – and she wishes she'd thought of it earlier.

She dozes, and wakes to find that they're trundling along a valley floor just outside Middlesbrough. It's dark now, and hills rise on either side with their tops still lit by the flattened rays of sunset. The sloping ground is littered with flints and criss-crossed by wavering drystone walls, and there's a cairn on the highest hillside. It's a tottering pile of rocks that catches the sun with a reddish glow and sends a shadow stretching like a finger towards the road. She rings the bell hurriedly and hopes the bus stop is nearby.

She'd thought she would recognise somewhere, remember something, but the bus has come to a juddering halt, and there's nothing left to do but climb down and stand under the fluorescent tube of the bus shelter. She's stiff now – too many hours on that seat – and her jauntiness has ebbed away to leave a strange, spreading misery. She's small again, she thinks; she's frozen and brown; she's fancy foreign muck.

The hillside rises gently, close-cropped grass scattered with rabbit droppings just becoming visible in the pallid moonlight. There's a remembered taste in that rising wind: Royapuram harbour after a storm. It's an old taste, a salt-and-decay taste of storms and weed and ocean slime, and murky waters covering things best left forgotten. Cars roar past on the road below. She's high enough that their lights only catch the edge of her coat, and she thinks with pleasure that she must resemble something quite natural – a rock, a tree – and not Deepa at all.

She reaches the cairn, still warm from the sun. Round the leeward side it's windless and calm, and she lowers herself down against the stones. The air here is quiet, and the grass has grown rank in long, weed-like strands that break under her fingers. The rocks against her back are colder than she'd thought, and feel less secure. Like the drystone walls – like a lot of things built to last – there's nothing holding them together.

Just over that rise, she thinks, there could be a little rocky gully with a bubbling stream and a crushed smell of clover and that miasma that rises from the grass at night. She could walk to the very edge of the cairn's long shadow and tug off her shoes, barefoot in the warm dust in the way she remembers. She could wade along the river, past the sharp-edged stones, and the silvery tadpoles and the splash and gurgle of great eels, past the bow waves of gigantic fish, past the worms hundreds of metres long and the flattened serpents that churn and coil in the current. She could be swept off her feet by the tidal surge, swept over a bottomless chasm of water the exact colour of her monster's tail.

She pulls her sari straight and settles back further in the grass. She has some things to leave, and here's as good a place as any. She doesn't expect to miss them, but just for a second she feels strange. Like a lemming, she remembers thinking a long time ago. Like a suicide pact. Like a village girl in a mango tree.

And so she leaves a sea monster here, under the stones where she can hide until her skin gleams new as copper. She leaves a bride, dressed in red and gold and all the colours of the sun. She leaves Annie, who's never seen a hospital trolley in her life; and Alex, who loves Sara and always will; and Anil, who came back from the navy and wrote them every single day.

It must be an hour later by the time Deepa stands up. The wind has risen, and she begins to feel her way through the flints to the bus shelter below. Bill will be wanting his dinner, she thinks, and starts to count ingredients in her head. One egg, two eggs. Suet for the jam roly-poly.

Rock Pools

I live in a city of widows, a grey town that clings to the rocks and cliffs of Northumberland like a spider on silk. Every year the storms bite away a bay or a stretch of sand. And soon, I suppose, they will bite away the widows.

Not everyone here is a widow, of course. But there's an enclave of us, hidden away behind closed front doors. Our hours are marked by laundry and cups of tea and the way the sunlight slants through the quiet dust of a kitchen window. Melissa next door, in a house the colour of caramel and barley sugar, is widowed every day by the eight-fifteen train to Edinburgh. And what does it matter if each night resurrects the husk of her husband from the station's treacherous platforms?

"What have you done with yourself all day?" he asks, coming out of the night to Melissa, bringing the ghosts of salt and seagrass into her caramel home. One day, I know, Melissa will tell him. But not today. She's too canny for that.

The dawn chill slides over my skin as I lean out of the window. Another morning; there's always another. Seagulls circle overhead, shining as they swoop through the yellowing light.

I pull on a chunky cardigan and old jeans, stiffened with salt and sweat. A ring winks at me from layers of tissue on the desk, but I shut the door firmly. Not this morning, I tell it; this morning I have no time for quagmires of the heart.

By the time I leave the house the sky to the east has turned a brazen pink, ripped by a golden crack. The seagulls are already wheeling across that rent, stitching it together with powerful wingbeats. They're watchful – at least where the widows are concerned – and a good thing, too. A sunrise like this could incite a woman to anything.

The gulls have been on this coast for years, long before widows or wives or husbands. There's a local legend that St Cuthbert conjured them up; called them out of sea foam to join him on the jagged Lindisfarne rocks. I wonder what he said to them in that new-hatched, washed-clean morning? I poke a toe into the damp sand, considering. Unlike Cuthbert, I have very little to say.

The birds lance upwards on spears of damp wind as I approach. All night they've been watching us, keeping the sea's bridal foam from our dreams. In India they used to throw the ashes of burnt widows into the water. They don't do that here, but perhaps the sea remembers. Those seagulls are our guards, flapping wings and glinting eyes to warn us against dissolving in the muscular waves.

As I turn back, the seaweed under my feet releases a whiff of salt and decay. The tide has changed, and a tongue of water laps between my legs. I briefly taste the chill of polar ice.

In town that morning there's a stir, a sizzling undertow to our usual work chatter. Something has happened.

"The scientists are here again. Came this morning." Annie beats the disapproving wings of her shawl as she settles herself behind the post office counter.

"Really? I thought they weren't coming this year." My voice is light as the sun on water. But the summer tides in Northumberland are treacherous; Annie knows this, and she doesn't approve.

"Jon's with them. Your *husband*." Oh yes. My husband, in as much as a ring in tissue paper and a thousand broken promises make a husband.

"That's nice." I shrug, turn easily away to sell some stamps to a dithering customer. What else would you like, Edith? What d'ye lack, what d'ye lack? Peel an apple on Midsummer Eve and it'll tell you, though you might not like the answer. "I haven't seen him since last year."

Jon comes every year, with the spring tide. The first time, five years ago, we came together. He set me down in our newly-wedded nest on the clifftop, and then he left next morning. Like Melissa's husband, who leaves her caramel house at the whistle of a train, or Edith's husband who arrives in her dreams but has never come in daylight, never.

Jon only left to study the birds. He observed; he recorded; he explained. And every night he returned and observed a dusty shelf here, a snappish word there. He recorded these things in his beak-sharp mind, weighed them up one against another. And one morning when the sky was peach and heavy and should have been beautiful, he began to judge.

Firstly, he explained that I clearly didn't love him, and perhaps never truly had. Untrue, but unarguable; how would I even begin? He was returning to London, he explained, to think things over. To dust his own shelves, spend evenings in an immense and silent peace. And then he'd come back, when it was time for the spring study of the birds.

And he did just that, flying off straight as a seagull into that peachy sky. He observes things, Jon: sea-birds, wives. I wonder if he gets it right about the birds?

Later that night I do my rounds, padding out onto the beach again. It's almost dark, but there's still a glow in the sky like a reminder of skin. The Farne Islands are jagged lumps of blackness against a murky sea and there's a tang in the air and a taste of devils on my tongue.

The seagulls sleep on the sand, preparing to guard us from whatever witchery the night might bring. They'll rise on silent wings at around three o'clock, with the first faint whispers of the tide, and they'll ride the waves till dawn. The locals call them Odin's crows, messengers from the gods. Jon, more reasonably, knows them only as *Larus Argentatus*.

Light puddles out from the hotel on the foreshore. There's music, and noise, and shadows pass and re-pass in front of the windows. A silhouette appears, sharp against the rosy light. Jon; I know his outline by heart. I step back, startled, slipping on the mossy rocks and scraping my feet on barnacles, but it's too late. He's seen me, and I feel the tide starting to turn, the current pulling urgently between my legs. It's too early, I think in panic, but when I look around, the gulls are already gone.

When I go for my walk in the morning he's already on the beach. Studying the birds, tagging them, assigning meaning to every flight. I've seen these seagulls every morning, could tell him all that he wants to know. Or perhaps not; we widows look at the world edge-on, and that's no use to science.

"Lisa." His voice is sunshine on sand. "I knew you'd be here."

Jon hasn't changed; he's still a length of copper wire, a current in my heart. He's slender, his hair glints gold and his skin is as brown as a duck's feather. Perhaps it's only widows who age. He walks closer – three, four strides – and takes my hands tightly in his. Around us, the gulls circle in a pattern of aggrieved surprise. *Touch a widow?*

He grins, jerking his head towards them. "They're getting ready to fly. It's why they're so jumpy."

"Jon," I say again, tightly, my fingers pinioned in his. "Let me go. I have to go to work."

He nods, slowly, and I snatch my hands back.

"You're not wearing your ring." There's a rip in his voice, something hurt, and I resist the urge to soothe. I'm no seagull, when I stitch up wounds it always leaves a mark.

"The ring gets in the way when I do housework," I tell him instead. It doesn't, of course. I used to wear it like a little collar of gold until a few months ago, when I first stepped out of the house in the clear bright morning to see the gulls.

He sighs. "I'm sorry, Lisa. Could we… would you have dinner with me tonight?"

I'm surprised. This isn't how it usually goes. We do talk, on his yearly visits. We sit over civilised glasses of wine and discuss his academic success – considerable – and my future – less certain – and once, awkwardly, whether I should go back to London with him. We agreed it was best that I stay. How strange, to agree something without saying a word.

Later that night we share a bottle of bitter white wine. Jon's words spin out into the night. *Try again*, he says, and *making it work* and *if you loved me*. I'm tired, and my heart pulses with his breath. I thought I *had* loved him, I thought we were in the past tense by now, but perhaps there's a distinction I'm missing. His eyes move like wings above a beach, snatching my secrets away.

I take his hand and feel salt in a fine grit against my fingers. And that night, for the first time in months, I don't listen for powerful wingbeats against the moon.

At sunrise Jon lies washed up on my bedsheets like flotsam on the morning tide. A pulse in his throat throbs and flutters. He's swooped in like a shower of gold, like a ravisher, like a guardian with pinion feathers of sea foam. Outside, the gulls are quiet.

He watches me get dressed, watches me put on my ring. It's not a decision, not quite. It's an easy way out. At work, Annie notices it, of course, and there's a glint in her magpie eyes.

"I see you two have made up! Good. A wife should be with her husband." She leans close, her shawl billowing and a puff of talcum rising from the salty hollows of her body.

"You take care though. It's a sight easier to tie a knot than free it, and you can strangle in the doings."

Annie isn't usually given to gnomic utterances. She dismisses me with a regal wave of her hand, an echo of her days as a Pearly Queen. Her talons cut off my unasked questions, and I open my mouth to see them float like incense over the town. What d'ye lack?

That night, the sky darkens with another storm. The air tastes of metal and brackish water and birds pace restlessly on the shore. It's a night for witches and secrets, for devils to skip our hearts over the waves. It's a night to lock up the widows, in case we decide to walk right out of our houses and swim until we find the morning.

Jon's in the house when I come back. I walk up the crooked path, puddled with light from the windows that falls on marjoram and seagrass. Inside I see Jon move easily from one room to the next, a shadow that flits across the herbs. It reminds me of a pair of gulls we watched together that first year. The male came back to the beach in spring, cocky and charming on a puff of warm air and headed straight for his mate. She was one of the few gulls who stayed on the beach over winter. Her wing was broken, years ago, and it ended her days of flight with him.

I decide to tell Jon this. But I don't tell him which bird he reminds me of.

After a month my house is changed. Things have moved, slabs of my life easing apart to admit Jon's solid passage. The light in my kitchen no longer marks the hours as they pass. A corn-coloured hair lies on my pillow, and a circle of gold winks on my finger like a band around a cormorant's neck. One day, I realise that the birds don't wake me anymore. I'm not surprised; the gulls only care for widows.

Jon tells me about them at night. "You see, Lisa, what we're observing is a new migration pattern."

A pause.

"The birds are being driven by hunger. That's why they're staying here so long."

Another.

"They've become dependent on people to feed them. Too many frustrated women in this place with nothing to do but throw breadcrumbs out of the window."

He wants to fight; he's picking at quarrels and snapping at silences. I feel sorry for him; all he wants to do is sink his teeth into flesh. But I can't oblige, not these days. These days, I don't even wake with the change of the tides.

A few weeks later his eyes begin to shift. Shadows on the beach again, shapes under water and a wind pushing foam towards me.

"Lisa, you know I'll be leaving in a week."

I nod. There are no birds left untagged, no flight patterns he hasn't recorded. There are no more questions, and there are too many answers. What d'ye lack, Jon?

"You'll stay here, of course." He pauses, uncomfortably. "But I won't be back again."

There are fish that live in rock pools constantly filled by the tide. They live and breed and die without ever seeing the ocean. They're beached, but their whole life passes without knowing it.

"I see." The smell of brackish seawater creeps into the kitchen, dank and wet.

"The study's finished, you understand, and…" He tails off. He wants to say I don't love him, but Jon hates to repeat himself. "I don't think I love you anymore."

Oh. Well, at least that's new.

We're very calm that evening. Jon observes my migration patterns from the living room to the kitchen. I'm being driven by hunger, and silence, and by the way the moonlight slants through the dusty window.

That night he reaches for me under our quilt. I move against him, slippery as a beached fish while he plunges and pecks at my body. He's brave, Jon. He tries, even when there's nothing left to try.

I'm woken by the sun, rising behind an ocean surge. My jeans are still stiff with salt, and tighter than they'd been. I leave Jon sleeping and go downstairs, where everything's oddly bright. The cliffs swim in a burning haze and the sands are pearled with dew. The gulls are waiting for me, clustered by the water's edge with wavelets lapping at the narrow bands around their legs.

I take a step and then run, pounding over the wet grey sand. The gulls squawk, fly up in panic and swoop away. And I turn back, too, back to my house with its brackish smell of seawater, and to my own narrow band.

I come down again that evening, and the next, and the next. The sun casts needle-thin shadows over the seagrass meadows as I run, leaping over the rock pools where fish live on land. The seagulls rise in panic, leaving this city of widows to our sea foam, and our throbbing darkness and our gleeful knowledge of what we lack.

Acknowledgements

Thank you to my husband, Paul, for his unfailing support, for his technical assistance and for being that rarest of beasts: a mathematician who speaks in music.

Thank you to my parents, Drs Alex and Nanda Menon and my brother, Anand Menon, for their encouragement and inspiration.

To Farhana Shaikh, of course, a champion of diverse voices in UK publishing, who seems able to cram 25 hours into every day.

To all at Dahlia Publishing, for their editorial and technical support with bringing this work together.

And finally, to everyone who's critiqued any of these pieces, from my MA classmates to my brilliant writing group, The Whole Kahani. To everyone at the Word Factory, for their inspirational events and short story workshops. To Steve and Bianca Emberson, Penny Canning-Menon and all at City University.

About the Author

C. G. Menon has won the Bare Fiction Prize, the Leicester Writes Prize, The Short Story Award, the Asian Writer Prize, The TBL Short Story Award and the Winchester Writers Festival award. She's been shortlisted for the Fish short story prize, the Short Fiction Journal awards, as well as the Willesden Herald, Rubery and WriteIdea prizes and the Fiction Desk Newcomer award. Her work has been published in a number of anthologies and broadcast on radio. She is currently studying for a creative writing MA at City University and working on her first novel.